NICOSIA BEYOND BARRIERS

Nicosia Beyond Barriers

Voices from A Divided City

Edited by
Alev Adil
Aydın Mehmet Ali
Bahriye Kemal
Maria Petrides

SAQI

SAQI BOOKS
26 Westbourne Grove
London W2 5RH
www.saqibooks.com

Published 2019 by Saqi Books

ISBN 978 0 86356 674 5
eISBN 978 0 86356 305 8

Cover image © Alev Adil

A full CIP record for this book is available from the British Library.

Printed and bound in Great Britain by Clays Ltd, Elcograf S.p.A.

This publication has been supported by Commonwealth Writers,
the cultural initiative of the Commonwealth Foundation.

CONTENTS

CONTENTS

INTRODUCTION

By Bahriye Kemal

At the crossroads of the world between west and east or north and south, Cyprus is a strategically located Mediterranean island that has had a distinct experience of major world events. It was once a transit site for Western pilgrims en route to the holy land, later an essential passageway towards conquest for Western and non-Western imperial regimes, more recently a key site associated with the Arab uprisings, with Islamic State activity and mass migration. The island has been subject to a cultural and political history of colonisation, partition and conflicting identities. At the centre of this make-up stands Nicosia, the world's last divided city.

This anthology aims to bring writers and poets together in a single volume that captures Nicosia as a shared and contested site, with dominant and marginalised narratives, capturing its fragments and its unities. The forty-nine contributors – well-known and lesser known writers and poets, as well as emerging voices – come from a variety of backgrounds. Some are from or now live in Cyprus, others are visitors who have been inspired by the island in general and Nicosia in particular. All have worked, performed, walked, written and lived through Nicosia. This anthology captures a new way of reading and writing not only about Nicosia, but also other cities that have been marred by colonialism, conflict and division. This anthology is a dynamic, all-inclusive platform open to diverse voices, which come together to use literature as a tool to capture solidarity and celebrate difference in the Mediterranean capital city of Cyprus. It is writing that freely travels through the world's last divided capital, bringing together strangers to create a new narrative of a city beyond all borders, boundaries, binaries, barriers.

ON HISTORICAL-POLITICAL NICOSIA, ΛΕΥΚΩΣΙΑ, LEFKOŞA: NAME GAME

This capital city has been a host to so many names throughout the ages. All the names of these different stages of the city's timeline will be voiced in this book. You will encounter various different names used for the same people and places, and here I will briefly explain the reasons through what I call the 'name game'. The name game is a core motif in cases of postcolonial partition – especially in former British colonies like Cyprus, Israel-Palestine, Ireland, India – that is commonly adopted by inhabitants of divided cities. This is a historical-political name game related to 'identity', most often based on ethnic, religious and/or national naming that divides groups of people into homogenous units. In these partitioned cases names consistently change when self and spatial conceptions change. In Cyprus this change operates as a site of contestation within and between 'Turkish and Greek', the dominant right-wing nationalist identifications that ideologically divides the people and places, and 'Cypriot', an emergent left-wing identification with a 'structure of feeling' towards uniting the people and places, ending in the adoption of 'Turkish-Cypriot' and 'Greek-Cypriot' as standard official names. In this book the preferred usage for the people of Cyprus would be 'cypriot', or to do away with binary names, however the contributors use binaries for clarification purposes. Here, you will encounter various different names for the people of Cyprus, including Turkish-Cypriot and Greek-Cypriot, cypriotturkish and cypriotgreek, T/Cypriot and

G/Cypriot. You will also encounter various different names for the same places, the most obvious to begin with being Nicosia (English), Λευκωσία/Lefkosia (Greek), Lefkoşa/Lefkosha (Turkish). In this way the book highlights and exposes the name game by showing that those of us who have felt partition, pain and wars are urged to play with and against naming conventions.

Thus in solidarity with the greatest philosophers and cultural theorists of our time, including Jacques Derrida, Paul Gilroy, Stuart Hall, Edward Said and Raymond Williams, who concern themselves with the name game as related to 'identity', this process reveals the following: an absolute rejection and weariness concerning the use of proper names for people and places; the farce of using a fixed, reified name for 'identity' (farcical because 'identity' is fluid); and the foolishness of notions like 'problem of identity' (foolish because 'identity' is not resolvable). There is no such thing as identity with a single name, there is only identification with multiple names. Identifications cannot and must not be considered via proper names because they lead to improper circumstances: it is those imaginings that prioritise ethnic identification over being an islander, or that prioritise identity to make it the higher, proper or uppercase, that have been the central culprits for the legacy of bloody binary contests and conflict in cases of partition. In this way the book captures and celebrates multiple different names for the city and its people that are always in production, so as to move beyond binaries and barriers.

This name game has been strengthened because of Cyprus's strategic position between the geo-political world divide, where it has repeatedly been at the mercy of various ruling regimes who have changed the name to assume ownership of the city, the island and its inhabitants. The Venetians built the city's walls with their 11-pointed bastions from 1489 onwards; the Ottomans took it in 1570 after posting their flag that transformed the city with new names; the British re-named it in 1878 via Herbert Kitchener's first comprehensive British-Cyprus map. By 1950-1960s the inhabitants sought to rename and reclaim their city, when the anticolonial campaign with competing moves mapped a Greece-Cyprus or Turkey-Cyprus. This paved the way for independence in 1960, when inter-ethnic conflict reigned. The 'Green Line' Agreement, when General Young drew the green ceasefire line that partitioned the city and its people in two, was drawn up on 30 December 1963 between Greece, Turkey and Britain. On 20 July 1974 Cyprus's geographical borders were reconstructed by Turkey through an extension of the Green Line that partitioned the people into ethnically homogeneous units, with the cypriotgreeks transferred to the south, and cypriotturks to the north. The borders then remained closed until Annan Plan V, a United Nations proposal that sought a resolution of the conflict before Cyprus's accession into the European Union. This resulted in the opening of the borders in 2003, with the intention to build up relationships in preparation for the referendum. There was no resolution. Cyprus today has the world's only divided capital with the south a recognised European state inhabited mostly by people who speak Greek, and the north a de facto entity mostly with Turkish speakers. Because of this spatiality, Cyprus is simultaneously at the centre and periphery of various positions that disturb fixed categorizations, thus serving to blur the dominant geo-political binaries within the city, the island and the world.

This spatiality is most prominent in the capital city, where it mostly operates through a dominant historical-political competing narrative between the cypriotgreeks and cypriotturks that generated the deadlock, which has come to be called the 'Cyprus problem'. This spatial history also operates via marginalised narratives, especially the literatures of Cyprus, so the literary Other that is largely excluded in a national and international domain, yet that must be selected as the preferred means to write and read the divided city, because it captures solidarity to create a differential island and city beyond all deadlocks and barriers.

LITERARY NICOSIA, ΛΕΥΚΩΣΙΑ, LEFKOŞA

The island and its city have always been a host for differential inspiration for the inhabitants, visitors and exiles who come here. It has created people and been created by people, triggering the act for all of us to write, read and construct it regardless of who we are, where we come from, or where we are going. In writing, reading and constructing the city we understand what it means to be at the crossroad of the world, fractured, to be postcolonial, European but not quite, Islanders, to be Muslim but not quite, to be Mediterranean, to be divided, to be united, to suffer in pain and longing together in solidarity. In this way we understand what it is to feel, live and create a city and be created by a city – a literary-lived Nicosia, Λευκωσία, Lefkoşa – that is host to total difference and diversity. To understand the overwhelming importance of the writings in this anthology, it is very important to consider the broad scope of writings about the city and the island that are not in this anthology. We must address the literatures of Cyprus within a colonial, postcolonial and partition framework, unpicking the official and dominant, as well as the unofficial and marginalised voices from the city. This will demonstrate the move from official nationalist writings that are exclusive, homogenous and/or hostile, towards the marginalised and unofficial writings that are inclusive and that celebrate the diversity and differences of the city. In this book there is a dynamic dialogue where these writers negotiate with the official nationalist and unofficial marginalised writings related to the island and its city that have gone before them.

To understand these writings, first it is important to mention that the divided island and its city are predominantly discussed in political and historical narratives, and the literary narratives are largely excluded. In more official contexts, the literatures of Cyprus are ethnically and linguistically divided as either Greek by cypriotgreeks or Turkish by cypriotturks. Through a comprehensive survey of the literatures, however, I argue that the literatures of Cyprus include writings in Greek, Turkish, English, Arabic and beyond by Cypriots – cypriotarmenians, cypriotmaronites, cypriotgreeks, cypriotturks – as well as by Greeks, Turks, Brits and others. These are simultaneously exclusive nationalist and inclusive transnational literatures; they are Cypriot literatures positioned between Greek, Turkish and English literatures, so multilingual, uncanonised and minor literatures between major literatures. I call them colonial and postcolonial diasporic writings operating within and through displacement. This is writing made up of various literary forms that focus on moving around and narrating the city and the island so as to narrate the self. This is writing about places, spaces and identification, which responds to the cultural and political history of colonialism, postcolonialism and partition-moments detrimental to the city and the island.

During the anti-colonial moment, the cypriotturkish and cypriotgreek ethnic-nationalists competed to write the city via ethno-religious affiliations, exclusivity and homogenisation, which generated the dominant and official narratives shaped by a wide selection of renowned works. Such pioneering works include Costas Montis's *Closed Doors,* which constructs the city of Λευκωσία through an ancient Greek spirit that maps a Greece-Cyprus, whilst Ozker Yasin's poetic legacy builds the city of Lefkoşa via the Ottoman martyrs' blood that poured into the city like a torrent during the conquest, so as to map a Turkey-Cyprus. In the postcolonial moment, after independence in 1963, literary works like Ivi Meleagrou's *Eastern Mediterranean* capture the failures when ethno-religious conflict reigned. Since partition, the city has maintained its significance in Cypriot narratives, where Niki Marangou's poetry – *Nicossieness* and *Selections from the Divan,* for example – capture the everyday life and death of diverse spirits, where childhood memories and other spirits move through the festivals and necropolis of the city, giving her the rightful title of poetess of Nicosia. This city has also hosted various diasporic groups, including not only renowned Cypriot figures – especially Aydın Mehmet Ali, Alev Adil, Stephanos Stephanides, Nora Nadjarian, Miranda Hoplaros, Andriana Ierodiaconou, to list a few – but also renowned migrants, exiles and diasporic figures like Palestinian poet Mahmoud Darwish, the Syrian Kurdish poet Salim Barakat and the Nigerian novelist Chigozie Obioma, who have led the way to capture the city with and through its division, diversity and difference.

This anthology writes back, with and through the aforementioned literatures of Cyprus and the city so as to be the first collection to capture fully this diversity in an all-inclusive and worldy way. It is made up of a wide selection of literary forms, which demonstrate the ways that writing Nicosia results in writing beyond barriers of literary conventions. Here the reader will encounter poetry, prose, prose-poetry, photo-poem, short-stories and plays that are fictional and non-fictional, which gives way to an intersection of genres – a hybrid intergeneric traffic.

Readers will encounter a polyphony of voices, which include the women of Literary Agency Cyprus (LAC) who organised the writing-walking workshops which began this collection's story, and/or various other literary and arts events organised by LAC. This anthology also negotiates with multiple voices from both or all sides of the Cyprus divide, which includes binaries such as the cypriotgreek and cypriotturk, the north and the south, the left and the right, the city and the country, the dominant and the marginalised. It also moves beyond Cyprus's binaries, capturing the marginalised position of people, poets and writers in various different contexts. This includes the position of the cypriotarmenian people, as in Aydın Mehmet Ali's 'My Accordion Teacher'. It includes poets from different territories such as Africa or India, who share a colonial and postcolonial history with Cyprus, as in Laila Sumpton's 'Nursery Tales'. This also includes the position of refugees, as seen in Melissa Hekkers's 'Island in the Sun', displaced university students, as in Tinashe Mushakavanhu's 'Nicosia's African Diaspora', exiled Arabs who experienced the Nakba and Israeli invasion who speak in my 'Spatial Tripling-Triad', and LGBTQ narratives, as captured in Stavros Stavrou Karayanni's 'Gardening Desire'. Nicosia is also written from various professional perspectives and disciplines, such as the architect in Adrian Woolrich-Burt's 'Flaş', the painter in Angus Reid's 'In The Company of Birds', the anthropologist via Yiannis Papadakis's 'Story/Language of the Dead Zone', the musician and rapper in Haji Mike's 'The Photo – The Guard Post', and numerous other perspectives, such as the post-colonialist, ethnographer and rhythmanalyst to list but a few.

These writers also imagine and live the city from the vantage points of those who roam Nicosia's streets. These include a tour guide, pilgrim, stalker, a feminised flaneur, a radical on a protest march, a vagrant caught in the rain, a ghost hunter and the hunted. Thus, these walkers – Andriana Ierodiaconou's 'The Heart of Nicosia', Marianna Foka's 'First Call', Stephanos Stephanides's 'Broken Heart', Dize Kukrer's 'The Endless Day', Dinda Fass's 'Calliope', Maria Kitromilidou's 'Beyond Barriers', Zoe Piponides's 'Hot City Dream' – set off without a map, itinerary, fixed starting point, destination or idea of how long their journey will take them, and only the beating pulse and rhythms of the city marks time passing.

Readers will walk through the city without a compass point, with frequent detours that go off the beaten track, moving beyond all signposts that mark the geo-political barriers.

In this book, the heart of Nicosia is captured in Venetian ramparts, British colonial parks, via ancient Greek gods, Byzantine saints, Ottoman baths, on balconies, and in the bookshops of the 1930s; in the taste of Lahmacun/Lahmajoun and souvlaki; in the scent of jacarandas, jasmine and cicada; in the voices coming from mosques and churches; under red flags, blue flags, white flags; and in all the varied daily practices within the streets of the city. Nicosia's beating pulse is often experienced through the practice of border-crossing and border-stopping at the immigration checkpoints, forbidden zones, or the dead zone between north and south Nicosia. Such border-crossing narratives were triggered by the opening of the borders in 2003 when all Cypriots were able freely to border cross to see places and people they had been prohibited from seeing for thirty years. The year 2003 became a moment where Cypriots partially replaced the 1963–1974 nightmarish stories with more positive 2003 stories of reconciliation. Such stories have not as yet been successfully institutionalised or nationalised, yet the narratives in this book capture fully that moment of possibilities. One pioneering text that captures this moment is Alev Adil's 'Fragments from an Architecture of Forgetting'. Other texts straddling this time include: Adrian Woolrich-Burt's 'Flaş', Haji Mike's 'The Photo – The Guard Post', and Maria Petrides's 'Coccinella, or Beyond Data'. Some writers have chosen to focus directly on the experience of border-crossing: Rachael Pettus's 'Ledra Street Crossing'; Kivanc Houssein's 'A Walk Through Ledra,' Nobert Bugeja's 'Ledra', Shola Balogun's 'I Too Shall Anoint the Stones' and Mary Anne Zammit's 'Shades of a City' come immediately to mind. These writers perform within the thriving-festering spaces of the dead or forbidden zones, buffering before the buffer zone, scratching at the neurotic act of border-crossing and re-crossing from one side of the divide and back again.

This crossing process also engages with time. On 30 October 2016, Turkey and the north of Cyprus opted out of the practice of Daylight-Saving Time, thus dividing the north and south of the island into two time zones. This inspired a new narrative among the people in Cyprus and the world as depicted in Antoine Cassar's 'Leaving Nicosia, Part Six (from Time Zones)', Argyro Nicolaou's 'A Waste of Time', Hakan Djumam's 'The Missing Hour' and Zoe Piponides's 'High Five'. The Nicosia experience and the way it has changed over the years depending on the political situation is further explored through pieces of writing that cover a significant lapse of time, such as Elisa Bosio's 'Blue Ants, Red Ants', Münevver Özgür Özersay's 'Buzzing Bees in my House', and Sherry Charlton's 'Nicosia Through the Eyes of a Child'. Through different generations, and joining writers at different points in their story, the reader feels what it is to be in Nicosia at different stages in the city's history.

Nicosia is likened to other former British colonial cities in Zimbabwe/Rhodesia in Caroline Rooney's 'Serendipity', and India and Palestine in Shereen Pandit's 'Divided Cities and Black Holes'. Going further afield, Nicosia as an 'other' city is given in Christos Tsiailis's surreal short story 'Knit'. Here, an alternate reality where giant roots strangle the buildings of the city and bind its inhabitants together in a shared semi-conscious stupor, induces the Nicosian experience. Nicosia is invented, un-invented and re-invented through architecture as in Christodoulos Moisa's 'Right-Hand Corner' and Sevina Floridou's 'Small Stories of Long Duration' and through language and translation, as seen in Stephanos Stephanides's 'Rhapsody on the Dragoman', Jacqueline Jondot's 'Why Are Green Lines Called Green?', and Yiannis

Papadakis's 'The Language of the Dead Zone'.

Thus, as a collection these works reveal the ways writing can move beyond dominant binary legacies of historical-political deadlock by creating a new literary form, language and geography, so that deeply divided and displaced inhabitants can speak to each other and to us about the important truths of Nicosia. These are truths that accommodate opposing forces, where the inhabitants are the victims and culprits of hostility, violence, pain, as well as advocates and opponents of the hospitality, peace and pleasures that make and break partition. This is a truth where global and local, powerful and powerless, rich and poor, marginalised and dominant actors can meet and speak so as to have a healthy relationship with the environment, which defines and disturbs the divided city and divided world. Thus Nicosia, Λευκωσία, Lefkoşa truths teach us about being citizens with and without the right to the city and the right to the world, where we can all conceive, perceive and live divisions, diversity and difference so to create a city and world without discrimination, where in solidarity we can live in longing for a transnational city and world beyond barriers that maybe one day will exist.

Nicosia Beyond Barriers

PAINTING IN THE WALL

Erato Ioannou

Psssssst ... psssssssssssssssssssst! Pssst!

Can you hear me?

Can you see me?

Crack of dawn marks my entrance to this world. Small colourful
drops sparkle in the moonlight. Pssssssst ... psssssssssssssssssssst!
A colourful mist of an umbilical cord connects us –

my creator and me – just for a short moment. After, the wall sucks
the colour in. And I become.

Smell of paint in my nostrils, oozing from the pores of my skin.
Hasty steps leave me at dawn. His backpack, hanging on his
shoulder, swings to the rhythm of his walk until his backpack,
and his hooded head, and his manly swagger melt in the hazy
contours of the city as humidity veils Nicosia in the young
hours of the day. His footsteps can be heard in the distance,
echoing against the walls, but not for long.

All I know is that I am. I am something. I am a thing inside a wall.
Spray painted. A work of art by an artist of questionable merit.

At nights I push. I push real hard, but it's no use. I push in spite
of that. My palms go numb against the sturdy cement surface.

'Hey, Kid! You on the opposite wall! Yes, you with the giant head
and big teary eyes. Can you hear me? Can you see me?'

In the mornings, dogs pee on my feet. The smell of urine masks
that of paint, momentarily. At nights, heated bodies press
against my flat embrace in the process of clumsy, rushed, upright lovemaking. Other times, hands press my cheek as they

lean against me for short moments of dull conversation. And I hear that they too are within a wall. Somehow forced to be there. Somehow, doomed.

'Psssst! Hey Kid? Here! Here, across from you! Have you ever tried?'

Kid's giant pupils, with honey-coloured highlights, glide to my direction – painfully slow.

'Have you ever tried to escape the wall? To walk out of it? Have you? Have you?'

Kid shows me two white teeth between a pair of fleshy lips – the smile of a teething infant. The kind of smile which could be a facial spasm, so beautifully captured underneath the skin, or a mere smirk of contempt.

At nights, I dream of earthquakes cracking the ocean's floor. Waves tower high into the sky, only to gash down into the bottomless void. Menacing rattle below the surface shutters the foundations. The walls crack. All of us glide through the crevices into the warm night – myself, Kid, Aphrodite and the giant sparrow, the woman with the white shawl. We walk unnoticed into the darkness – bodiless, non-existent. Trickles of paint mark our passage until, they too, vaporise into the paleness of the landscape at dawn.

Even in my sleep I push. The wall mocks me. Its surface turns into an elastic impenetrable membrane. I push. The membrane pushes me flat.

There must be something about walls and this town. Walls encircling her. Walls gashing across her. Walls. Walls are meant to protect. Am I supposed to be safe in mine? Shall I strive for escape never again?

There's this girl. She giggles and talks too loudly. She takes snapshots of the walls. I am used to this. If I could I'd strike a pose. She presses her back against my bosom and her skin feels so soft.

A drop of sweat trickles down her nape and in between her shoulder blades. Life is oozing through her and I want to suck it all in. I would kill her if I could – just for a short walk down the road, just for some giggles and a word or two too loud. If only I could be that girl! With flesh and bones and a heart pumping blood into my veins, free to walk the narrow roads without walls to hold me back.

My face shows next to hers on the rectangular screen of her phone. She smiles a wide smile. I have no mouth. I am gagged. Her skin glitters in the sunlight. My surface is rough and scaly.

At night, I think that maybe there is no use. What is the point. I am flat. Embedded. Bodiless. Gagged.

Psssssssssst. Psssssssssst ... pssst.

And the night is long.

Psssssssssssssssssst. Psssst ... pssst.

Endless

Psssssssssssst. Psssst ... pssst.

In the morning there is a new one next to Kid. He looks at me straight in the eye.

'Psssssssssssssssssst. Psssst ... pssst! You! Hey, you!' he hollers. 'Have you ever tried to escape the wall? To walk out? Have you? Have you?'

NICOSIA – WHISPERS OF THE PAST

Anthie Zachariadou

The cities of Europe are filled with whispers of the past and a trained ear can even detect the rustle of wings and the palpitation of souls and feel the dizziness of centuries of glory and revolutions ...

Albert Camus

In September 1955, the couple boarded a Cyprus Airways plane to Nicosia, a 15-hour trip with a stopover in Rome. All arrangements had been carefully made beforehand. Michael had thought that it would be best for them to live in close proximity to a good school and the Government House, in a nice little neighbourhood, which happened to be where his mother used to live.

Michael asked Barbara if she wanted to go and see the house where his mother had grown up. He was surprised to find that it had been recently vacated and was available to rent, and that is how, at the age of twenty-two, Barbara found her home. A semi-derelict semi-detached stone-build with a tiled roof, a world away from Cambridge. Located in a street fewer than three metres wide, if she stood in the middle with her hands stretched out she could almost touch the buildings on either side. It was both secluded and claustrophobic. Inside, a wooden door opened up to a yard of cobblestones and withered plants. Barbara smiled when she saw what seemed to be a toilet at the yard end corner. To her left was a closed door made from walnut wood. Barbara lost herself in ideas of what she could do with this place. She held Michael's hand as they walked around the neighbourhood, all simple, stone blocks stuck together; all so pretty, so obviously loved and cared for.

Grasping the hand of her ever-so English-looking husband, they walked on and found themselves gazing at a pretty church, similar to the chapels in Cambridge, but of a different rhythm – the Greek orthodox style. Michael explained that the church was dedicated to the patron saints of the neighbourhood, Ayii Omoloyitae. The saints' names were Gourias, Samonas and Avivos, and Barbara smiled at the sound of those names, remembering snippets from her childhood of her dad's Greek heroes whose stories she had not paid attention to. They walked on, passed through a few more tightly knit houses, and out into another opening. It was the smallest of squares framed only by a couple of coffee shops where old people sat doing nothing. What on earth were they thinking? In the middle, a huge sycamore tree stood, majestic and strong. She moved beneath its canopy to get some protection from the blazing sun. Carefully, she studied its strong dark trunk branches abundant with heavy leaves and she had a sudden yearning to paint it. She felt Michael smiling down at her, as he whispered, 'You will have ample time to paint it, my darling. Platanos has been here for centuries, it's not going anywhere'.

That is how Barbara started her life and built her home in Nicosia. She did actually renovate it herself. She discovered old wood workshops and carried planks, found out who sold varnishes and brushes, painted walls, had a new kitchen installed, scrubbed, brushed, sawed even, enjoying every minute of it. She uprooted the green remnants in the yard and planted Michael's favourites: sunflowers and geraniums, dandelions and lilies. She found that it wasn't difficult to move around the area, it was such a compact place. She bought a bicycle, taking what she needed with her.

The days passed peacefully. Michael was content teaching and Barbara, when she had finished restoring the house, took up painting again. She discovered a little art shop not far away where she could get most things, and her mother sent over parcels containing anything that she couldn't find. She turned the room with the walnut door into an art studio, and she also enjoyed painting outdoors. By Christmas she had completed portraits of the old lady living next-door to them and of the man around the corner, Mr. Costas, a shoe repairer, who could always be found sitting on his doorstep with his awls and scissors and someone else's shoe. The pretty chapel with the sculpted bell-tower and the school of Ayii Omoloyitae were her favourite places to paint. She had a folding chair and her easel and canvas and brushes were easy to take out, under the lovely blue Cyprus sun, in the comfort of a light breeze. She loved that she could walk around without worrying about catching a cold, how she would greet everyone who passed by and they would smile and look approvingly at what she was doing. Platanos was an ongoing project, she needed to make it perfect, so she took her time.

It took several months for Barbara to understand that she was not, in fact, in paradise. She had heard a few shots over the course of several days and caught worrisome words on the radio, but Michael always reassured her, talking of practice military runs, or some drabble between the Greek and the Turkish Cypriots. But as happens in all marriages, she got to know him. She noticed his eyes grow a touch sadder, heard anxiety not tiredness in his sighs. The excitement of teaching maths to eager students began to fade, and then she knew enough about him to understand that routine was not to blame, but something else. She did not want to ask her neighbours. They had bonded and she had painted their children and animals and gardens but she was still a foreigner to them and she did not want to hear the answers she did not want: not from them, not yet. She decided that she would pay more attention to the news and read the papers.

One day in 1956 she heard on the radio that an English student, Michalis Karaolis, had been hung for treason. Her heart stopped for a while. What could a twenty-two-year-old have done to deserve hanging? And then it wasn't hard to put together all the pieces she had chosen to ignore, to mature, to read in the look on her husband's face as he opened the door to their home that night that they were British people living on an island governed by British people, and that the Cypriots did not want them there.

She would never, she promised herself, *never* bother Michael with this. She would not spoil for him the dream that she was perfectly happy painting away, chatting with neighbours, cycling in the town, cooking, gardening, carefree, clueless. She felt that the only way she would help him was providing this distraction for him, the serene wife. She knew the dynamics of their marriage and she would play it right. She would be the little girl who could cheer the old man up. And Michael did seem to grow older by the day. With every explosion they heard, every time he returned from a 'late evening class' when she knew he had been summoned to meetings at the military headquarters, with every slight noise, every start of every news story on the radio, Michael's eyes appeared more wrinkled, lines forming underneath them, creases around his mouth. But her duty was to stay young for him. So she did.

She asked him nothing, and pretended that everything was fine, even after they attended dinners with British officers and their wives, who were all making plans to return to the UK. But she did her own research, and she learned by chatting casually with the locals – from the girl who she bought pastries from at the *Mondial* sweet shop to the priest she ran into in the street whilst out walking. Pater Vasilis took her to see the old catacomb underneath the bell-tower, and there he explained, calmly, what was going on. The Greek Cypriots wanted to be real Greeks.

They wanted *enosis*. She wished she could call her father and ask him what that word meant, but now it was too late. He would worry and command her to come home. In every letter she sent to her parents she reassured them all was fine. How could she tell of Grivas and his fixation, the guerrilla fights or that some of Michaels's students had been involved in the escalating attacks against the British? By 1957, a Briton was attacked or killed every few weeks. Barbara concentrated on shaking off all uneasiness and upped her efforts to mingle with the Cypriot people. She needed to see if they all viewed her as an 'enemy' or if this was just a bunch of extremists, 'trouble-makers' as the governor had told her. Did they only hate the fact that they were under British rule or was there something else: a desperate need to be *real* Greeks, not Greek Cypriots, not Cypriots who spoke Greek?

She rode her bike to the Paphos gate one morning, and, as usual, passers-by greeted her warmly. She stopped at a bakery and bought a loaf of freshly-baked bread. She chatted to the owner in Greek, which, after almost two years on the island she felt she had mastered enough to hold a basic conversation. He replied in English, told her he was thinking of closing the shop down. No, he didn't hate them, he told her, ' ... of course I don't hate *you*, I like *you*, *kyria* Barbara ... But these kids are fighting for their ideals, they believe in something – do you know, *kyria* Barbara, that we Cypriots have done nothing, nothing all these years for freedom? We have always been captives of some nation or other. Did you know I'm seventy-eight years old, *kyria* Barbara, and this is the first uprising that I have seen?' Their conversation was interrupted by noises outside. They went out and saw a group of children throwing stones at a convoy of British government cars. She went closer to them and stood next to them. She felt the urge to share their passion, to be carried away in the excitement of the uprising, to join the cool crowd, as teenagers do, without grasping the significance. Barbara had olive skin and brown hair and eyes, unlike her husband. She was closer to the children in age than she was to other British officers' wives. When she joined them, they hardly gave her a second glance, but one of them handed her a stone and said '*Na fyoun oi skatoenglezoi, enosis!*' and then Barbara threw the stone, which missed the car and landed on the ground somewhere. She stayed, watching her country's vehicles quickening away with smashed windscreens.

MY ACCORDION TEACHER

Aydın Mehmet Ali

... vanished one day. I didn't understand it. Perhaps he did tell me he was going to vanish. Not come to our lesson. Perhaps he did tell me the reason, or perhaps, he tried to shield me from the real reasons, thinking I was too young to understand or be made a participant in grown-up things. But I did wait for him. I still practised madly, diligently the whole week, waiting to impress him as he had impressed me. I wanted to play just as well as he did. Smiling whenever he would skip the pages of my exercise book, right to the end and burst into amazing music I could listen to him breathless, with fluttering inside me, impatient for the time when I would play just like that without even looking where to place my fingers and deciphering the beetle-like legs crawling all over the pages of my exercise book. Not only that, but with a face lost in rapture in some other place than the muddy streets of my neighbourhood outside the Nicosia walls, imagining things I could not even begin to imagine ... I was ten, perhaps eleven. My mother had bought me the accordion because she liked the sound. Perhaps the melancholia of dancing with her husband. But it was about the tango. She was convinced that I would learn to play, and to love it, just as she did.

He didn't come. At first, I thought it incredible that he was not at our lesson at the arranged time. He used to come with a mobilette, one step up from a bicycle. I had everything ready. My music scores, the accordion out of its case, a chair and one for him in my mother's reception room, for guests only. He didn't come.

I went out to the front garden of our council house built by the Colonial Administration for low-income families in the service of the Empire. My mother a nurse at Athalassa Sanatorium; my father, dead.

Why didn't he come? I stood at the gate looking both ways, hoping to see him appear from around either corner. He didn't. I stood, stubbornly waiting as time passed. He didn't. My mother came out, 'He won't come,' she said, softly. Perplexed, I crossed my eyebrows even more than they were. A silent question, she understood. 'He won't come today,' she said, just as gently. She intercepted my why and told me in a hesitant voice that there was trouble, '... some are making trouble for some people,' she paused, 'who are not Turkish,' barely a whisper.

'But he speaks Turkish,' I say, indignant.

'But he is Armenian,' she said, 'he is not Turkish, and they know it.'

'So, what's wrong with that? He is my teacher. He was coming all this time ...?' rattles out of me, fast.

'Now, he can't come!' her voice adamant, doing battle with my stubborn glare directed into her eyes. Did she tell him not to come? Was she to blame? I was doing so well – he had told me so with a smile, the previous week. She gives in to my angry, questioning eyes.

'They won't let him,' she says so softly. Who? Who won't let him, I demand still glaring at her, silent. She knew I would do that.

'Some people don't want the Armenians, the Greeks, the Maronites amongst us. Look ...' with anger in her own voice now, her hand sweeps across the neighbourhood.

'They have all gone! Look at Maro, your best friend ... she's gone, overnight. She has disappeared. *Kyria* Maria is gone; they are both Greek, and the Maronite sisters from around the corner, the Latins from around the other corner, have gone. They've all gone!' and she walks back into the house exasperated. She is thirty-two and beautiful. Green eyes and thick chestnut hair, the nurse of the neighbourhood. Everyone willingly bared their bums for her to jab in her syringe of their medication. Mother of three, bringing them up on her own since the death of the man she could love only for four years. I am confused. Deflated, I walk back into the house after her, wringing my hands. She comes into the room, takes me into her arms. My head doesn't even reach the top of her breasts. 'It is not your fault,' she says. But I know it is not my fault! I don't say it, enjoying our intimacy. 'He wants to come, he thinks you are a good player but he can't come, now. Maybe ... Maybe later ... When things calm down; he will come.' I collude with the lie my mother tells me because I am desperate for it to be true. My willing collusion. He never came.

Later, I marvelled at how she kept it all together. A beautiful woman, friends with all those 'non-Turks' in the neighbourhood, their nurse when they needed her services. And all her friends and colleagues at Athalassa Sanatorium, where she worked, were 'non-Turks'. She was the only Cypriotturkish female nurse in the hospital.

She couldn't tell me, a child, that the TMT had threatened her, telling her she could not have an Armenian teach her daughter, just as they had driven out all other communities from our neighbourhood by 1958, using the Cypriotturkish children and young people of the neighbourhood and others, to stone and throw Molotov cocktails through their doors and windows. That my teacher had been threatened not to come to the neighbourhood. And I didn't know that Armenian shops were being looted, people threatened, prevented from going to work, told to leave and not come back. An ethnic cleansing had begun.

'We had no problems, between Turkish Cypriots and Armenian people. Not in this area,' she says. 'Nothing!' her voice authoritative, too sure of itself. My crossed eyebrows go into overdrive.

'Not so,' says the man sitting next to her, after some hesitation, who knew more of the TMT activities, as a man above a certain age. I sit opposite him focused on his searching, saddened eyes. Waiting for him or for someone else to continue. I so want not to be the one, yet again, to challenge this myth that everything was fine between us. We are in the garden of an old house, perhaps abandoned by an Armenian, renovated with the help of EU and USAID funding. I respect her. We had been part of a women's oppositionist group, speaking out, in our long personal herstories. A morning glory vine climbs the body of a date palm in the middle of the garden, while a German woman pulls up its suckers from the earth. In the corner, two young mulberry bushes barely carry their sparse, newly-ripened white fruit, a lemon tree has scattered a few lemons onto the ground and the young woman from Turkey, who in partnership with the young woman from Armenia, has made a short film about students and their perceptions of each other within a German-funded project, picks up some lemons and puts them in her bag. She has a heavy cold. Her throat shredded by an infection. There are others who are part of *Speaking to One Another Exhibition*, a collaboration of young university students from Armenia and Turkey.

Sirarpi get up! Get up!

What do you mean get up? I am dead!

Just get up, I tell you!

Now?

We have to go.

Go where?

We have to go to the old mahalle.

Old mahalle? What for? We left that long ago.

She is coming. She is there ... We have to go!

You, crazy old girl. We are both gone, we've long gone. You still talk about going to Arabahmet, Ani. You're crazy ... I should say, you haven't lost your craziness! Always like that, dragging us from one adventure to another... a miracle we didn't die young.

She is calling us...

Calling us? How? She can't even speak Armenian.

We speak Turkish, don't we? And she thinks more beautifully than the Cypriots do.

So?

So, we have to go! We have to help her.

Ani... Ani... we are old! W-e-e-a-re-o-o-old! Get that through your head! And leave me alone. I've done all my running around.

Sirarpi get up, she's calling. I can see her. She is sitting in the garden of Mama Ziljian's old house. With the date palm. Remember? We pushed the kernel secretly into the soil to spoil their immaculate garden... hahaha! Now it's grown.

Stop it Ani!

There are others. Some sort of gathering.

Stop! I am not moving. We are dead!

'Maybe we should start with food; we share that. We have so many dishes which are the same!' continued the woman I respect. Alarm bells ring in my head, deafening. No. No! We can't have the Cypriot version of the three Ss: Steel-bands, Saris and Samosas. We had all that in London in the late 1970s, early 1980s. As educational activists, we fought it. School 'multicultural' events required parents to come to special evenings, bring their food and artefacts, maybe do a dance, then go home. Involvement in curriculum development, appointing teachers, removal of racist books from the school library... was not allowed! Nothing would change; racism and prejudice would continue, power relations would remain unquestioned, unchallenged.

I squirmed in my seat. Food again! Dancing again! Artefacts

again! But that was thirty years ago in London! I listened. I watched the others in the group. Did anyone else feel discomfort? Were they too 'polite' to say something? Why are people colluding under the disguise of being polite?

'The Armenian Church should be opened for religious services, to become alive, that will bring the Armenian community back,' she says with the authority of one used to being unchallenged. Will it? I ask, with a crashed soul. Why should they come to the places from which they were driven out? What is there to come back to after fifty-five years? Would anyone want them back or welcome them? Would anyone be brave enough to challenge nationalism and Turkification, which forced them out? Why didn't the Cypriotturkish communities prevent their displacement? Why did we – am I part of this we, eleven at the time – collude in their expulsion? We were silent and still are, about past injustices. We present their departure from the Arabahmet neighbourhood, as a choice, which is immoral. We abdicated our responsibility for such actions and our role. We opted for selective memory, remembering and forgetting and blamed the victims.

I call them. Silently. Sitting in the middle of this garden. My eyes scanning the sky. Part exasperation, part seeking inspiration... imagination. I search the umbrella of fronds of the male date palm swaying imperceptibly high above.

What would they have made of all this? The women who lived here?

I scan the first-floor balconies, windows of the surrounding buildings, remnants of various architectural fancies and histories in degrees of neglect and collapse. My ears strain to hear Armenian. Is someone playing the piano? The accordion? Is someone singing? Who is speaking in Armenian? Who is responding in Turkish, the Italian of the Middle East, of the high cultured, educated of Adana, Antalya, Antioch, who arrived, just as the recent refugees from Syria, Palestine, Lebanon, Egypt and beyond, who had the means and connections to leave, to flee, to survive?

You getting up or what?

No!

You're always the same Sirarpi... No! No! You're so boring! Since we were kids!

Mmmm...

If it wasn't for me, you would still be in Turkey. And dead at the age of four! Remember that! Remember the soldiers? Remember, I pushed you into a big pot, in the pigpen! And climbed in after you! Remember? It was long ago, but you must remember that!

Mmmm...

And now get up! I'm losing patience! We're going!

Oh, come on. Pull me up... as time goes it gets harder to move. Especially getting up from horizontal.

Here, let me straighten you out a bit...

Stop fussing! There's nothing to straighten out! Here we are, wearing our silk tulles. Our most recent fashion statement. And most comfortable. I wish I had discovered this weightlessness earlier. What was that? The unbearable lightness of being... Kundera, I think.

Oh, stop showing off! We all know you read a lot. And you were a writer. Back to business.

Yes ... funny business! Now what?

We go and listen. See what she has in mind!

Yes ... minds, we can read!

'Food is not enough,' bursts through my lips, despite efforts to contain myself. 'I don't think we need to prove that we have common dishes in this part of the world. Why don't we do something, which will enable the Cypriotarmenian and the Cypriotturkish communities to lay claim to shared histories, presence, cultural heritage and economy in this neighbourhood? That we shared a life. We have deleted them from the history of this neighbourhood. Why don't we help reclaim that?'

Sirarpi! She's stopped!

They're shocked! She is right, Ani.

'Instead of bringing dishes of cooked food, why don't we ask them to bring their photos?'

So, she wants photographs.

Yes, photographs ...

And she wants to blow them up.

Yes, huge!

Yes, and hang them from the roof down, did she say?

Something like a huge scroll ... unrolling.

Yes ... So, she's going to hang us on the walls of our old houses?

Yes ... to make it visible that Armenians lived here, she said.

'So we can all celebrate and remember the people and lives lived and add photos of others – dead or alive. A way to claim our heritage, separately and together. Without fear...' rolled off my tongue, fully aware that the nationalists and emerging fascists would be on the streets, in no time, knifing, scratching, tearing and burning the photos.

I suppose that's the only way we're going back to our old houses ...

Ayo.

Evet! Yaa ... işte böyle.

We waited for so long to go back. There was never a way back, neither to Turkey, where we left everything, nor to our dead.

And neither to Arabahmet. At least we managed to save our lives and some of our belongings.

... and we stayed in one city; divided, but at least we knew it. It was home.

... and our friends and relatives and school and cemetery were in the city! We lost our homes. So, now what?

How can we claim there were no problems between Cypriotturkish and Cypriotarmenian communities? Did we even consider them as refugees? No one bothered to tell me they were from Turkey or tell me their stories. We marvelled at how beautifully they spoke Turkish, so much better than us, Cypriots. In the 1980s, I began to discover the buried herstories and the fall-out from the military dictatorship and the massacres in Turkey. Kurdish and Turkish communities I worked with, who had escaped to London, told me.

I came across Cypriot Armenians, soon after. I met Ani, filmmaker, intellectual, brave woman, speaking five languages, immense knowledge of the Middle East, with whom I became close friends, debating into the early hours of the morning; and later, her mother, Syrarpi, born in Mersin, Turkey and grew up in Cyprus. Her family was forced out of Turkey; she was forty days old. Their boat with hundreds of refugees was refused landing in Cyprus, by the British. She wandered the eastern Mediterranean for a month, refused at every port, before being allowed to dock back in Cyprus. Syrarpi told me, and more stories followed. Another herstory, completing the missing bits of my heritage, had opened up. She had lived in Nicosia.

Ani and Syrarpi came to stay with me in Nicosia around 2011. Syrarpi wanted to find her house in the North. Could I help? We walked the streets, holding hands, like two little girls on a treasure hunt, giggling. She held a tiny black and white, serrated-edged photo of a house with railings; I asked questions to jolt the nearly 90-year-old mind. But that wasn't the house, she said, but it was close by. I took her to the building; no reaction. After another hour of wandering around, all three brains scrambled in the heat, I asked her to imagine coming out of the house; what was opposite? A clinic. I knew it well. I took her to the old clinic, now a club for old TMT members, who forced the likes of her out of this and my neighbourhood. She looked carefully; blank face, no flicker of the eyes, confused, disappointed. I took them down the adjacent side street, along the wall. As we walked, Ani became animated, she kept repeating, 'it's here, it's here'. Syrarpi's eyes lit up with expectation, but unsure. In front of the side gate of the clinic, she nearly jumped. Her house was opposite. She burst into laughter, telling Ani, 'I told you so'. At five, Ani's memory went into overdrive when we entered the derelict building – a feeding-ground for cats and scattered empty food tins. They were both animatedly speaking over each other; I, trying to keep up with the images, actions, cooking, sleeping arrangements, uncles, aunties, cousins, rooms, garden, swings, games ...

I told them later that this was the clinic my mother was brought to by her father from the village, aged sixteen, and handed over to the doctor and his German archaeologist/painter wife, to be a 'helper'. Dr. Rauf and Olga. Her parents never came to see her. But the doctor taught her the basics of nursing. My mother and Syrarpi had lived five metres across the road from each other. My school was fifty metres from both. I marvel at such historical accidents that placed the three of us within this fifty metres of Nicosia and our future connections.

She walked us through the *mahalle* of her childhood until she left for Beirut, aged twenty-eight, pointing at each house, naming all who lived there. At times we sat on a wall so she could rest. She knew the wall. She kept patting it with her hands. Her eyes scanned everything. Old and new images rushing at her. Ani in total awe of her mother's memory and lucidity, now silent, listening. A humbling experience and privilege that I will carry.

Ethnic delineation, realignment, cleansing and borders led to the formation of enclaves by the Cypriotturkish power elites in the early 1960s, ruled by military commanders from Turkey. With self-rule, a captive, sole-use economic market and the superiority of the 'Turks' as foundations. The Armenians were rejected as Christians and targets of the genocide in Turkey, busy building the 'motherland' of all Turks. Maronites and Latins didn't fare any better. Muddling issues of race, ethnicity, religion and human compassion was not to be tolerated, and neither was their presence in the enclaves, especially as businessmen creating competition within the context of the *Türk'ten-Türk'e* (from Turk to Turk) campaign. The power elites forced them out, the rest of us colluded. What is not acceptable is that we have yet to apologise for our collusion in the destruction of their lives. They were seen as siding with the 'Greeks' and being ungrateful, especially when they took their money and their jobs and left.

They were not that welcome amongst the Cypriotgreek communities either. Careful not to take sides, their survival was precariously balanced, only finding safety amongst their own communities. Perhaps the eternal positioning of repeatedly displaced minorities, anywhere.

Now, we talk to those who have our photographs. Their walls and sideboards, shelves and albums are full of our photos. They look at them to remember us.

Yes... every-now-and-then.

Yes... now, we have to wait for them to come and visit!

When's the next time?

Don't know. When's your birthday? Do they come then? Mine's gone, and we can't wait for the next one!

Mine is in six months; no good!

Christmas? New Year? Assumption of Mary on 15 August, will it fall on that day this year? I can't keep up with the changes from one calendar to the other; Gregorian, Julian ... The months of the 1915 killings? Which day did they choose to remember our mothers and fathers and grandparents, and sisters and brothers, and uncles and aunties, and neighbours and teachers.

The list is long enough Ani. Ahhh... the genocide. Turkey is still in denial. Enough! We know the story; that's 24 April. Now we have to find some dates soon.

We're both losing it dear, our memory is not what it used to be, or we have become selective in what we remember and what we choose to forget.

Sometimes it's good to forget.

What it boils down to is that we have to send them messages. We'll talk to them when they come with bundles of flowers and dot them all around us.

They are so melancholic sometimes, especially my young grandchildren. I feel sorry for them. They've inherited a shitty world ... bok bir dünya, it's blowing up in their faces.

And, forget our children – they are useless! All they think about is getting on! On what? In a rat race. They have no time. They don't talk to their children; too busy. Let's talk to the young. At least they are curious about us, where we lived? How? History. Language. Stories. Culture. Music. Love. Jokes. Games we played as kids.

Now, they love the Tablet; it's a good name: the Pill! Yes, I'll talk to Nora. She comes, tells me things I suspect she doesn't tell others.

Talking is good...

And we'll have to make sure Simon finds the girl ...

Which Simon?

The journalist. He is active at the Club, you know ...

Ah yes ... And make sure the girl comes across our photos and those of others ...

Now, can we go? Haydi. I need to lie down. Don't forget I'm ninety-four and you're no spring chicken, at eighty-five. Do you think she'll make it? Have our photos on our houses?

I think she will try; she manages things others don't even think about ... How long? I don't know.

I've been walking and cycling this neighbourhood for half a century. I tell stories and listen to others. Paphos Gate to the Armenian Church, along Victoria and side streets, Arab Ahmet mosque, down to my school, up on the Venetian ramparts, the Latin and Maronite churches weaving in and out of abandoned, closed, derelict buildings, shops, workshops decaying for decades capturing slow decay in search of the Armenian script hidden above doorways stubbornly calling it the Armenian neighbourhood and not Arabahmet ... lest I forget; my individual rebellion. I see images, photos on those walls. Many come with me, a graveyard of past lives crowding my imagination while new inhabitants also from southern Turkey smile and the children race me with their bikes or want to ride mine.

This is where I went to Victoria Kız Lisesi (Victoria Girls' Lycée), founded in 1903 with thirty pieces of gold guineas, donated by Queen Victoria to educate girls; now Nicosia Turkish Girls' Lycee. Our excited laughter, screams, award ceremonies, pitches where we grazed our knees and arms diving for the ball, where we posed with cups and medals for volleyball and handball, my team the school champions, where our music room was devoured by fire and where we sang the national anthem with the flag of the Republic of Turkey on Monday mornings and Friday afternoons. Now it's a car-park. It was from here that I left for the US on a one-year scholarship, aged sixteen, never to return, courtesy of the same war that drove the Armenians out of our neighbourhoods. A loss I am still compensating for. I had to go search for it across the world and back.

And my accordion teacher? I asked many.

'He went to Australia, I think,' said Maluk, the old Armenian activist trade unionist, when we met on his balcony in the early 2000s, talking politics. 'He migrated in the early 1960s. There were assisted passages in those days.' He smiled, 'He was the only one who could play classical music on the accordion, in those days. The only teacher of the accordion,' with admiration in his voice. No, he didn't remember his name.

DIVIDED CITIES AND BLACK HOLES

Shereen Pandit

In Nicosia
They said I'd dropped
A man into a black hole in my brain
Forgotten him entirely
Deleted his existence

I began to look for him
With fingers feeling
Round the black nothingness
The no man's land of my mind
Wandering this side and that
Crossing and re-crossing the Green Line
From existence to non-existence and back
Searching
For a life
A human life I'd lost.

Perhaps, I thought
He'd be in Jerusalem
Perhaps he'd be in Cape Town
Those other divided cities I have loved
Perhaps I lose people
Down black holes
In every place which belongs to no man

FLAŞ

Adrian Woolrich-Burt

The flash lit up the night sky like a cannon shell. 'There is no way we are going to get away with this,' thought the Anthropologist, 'not here'.

It wouldn't have been correct to say that the Marxist was unperturbed, she looked unperturbed and she still spoke in a half-whisper, as did he, but her words came out shorter, more clipped and the tone went up an octave at least.

They carried on chatting, sotto voce, about the war in 1974, about the fact that most people in the West thought that was the start of it and the Green Line had been drawn at this time, at the ceasefire – and it hadn't, it had been drawn long before, in the mid-1960s, and drawn in people's mind long before that. They carried on chatting but not in the same way, not after the flash, they couldn't, it was only a matter of time.

The Anthropologist listened to what she said, intently. It was too dark to make notes, his field notes, but he wanted everything to be noted down, logged, documented. What had Malinowski said? Rather what had his academic supervisor said that Malinowski had said ... write everything down, everything, you don't know what is going to be useful until you have everything, and until you have everything you don't have anything that's useful. The Marxist was speaking about the plans for a new hotel. She wasn't in favour. That was no surprise, she was a Marxist. The Anthropologist caught up, skipping over Malinowski, like you could on an old VHS by keeping the play button down and then pressing the fast forward, you can't do that on a DVD so easily, or perhaps you could – he'd have to remember to ask someone. If he had his field notebook that would go on the inside back cover, at the bottom of the list headed 'Notes and Queries'. Malinowski, black and white photo sideways on, he was famous for taking anthropology off the verandah, but that's the famous photo of him isn't it, on the verandah? Or perhaps that's Evans-Pritchard? No he thought, no verandahs in the Sudan, it's Malinowski, in jodhpurs and pith helmet taking anthropology off the verandah. What pompous clap-trap – the Anthropologist's wife had once told him about an exhibition at the Wellcome Collection which explained how Malinowski had really spent a lot of his days drinking cocktails with the white missionaries, and rather more of his evenings bonking the natives. That was one aspect of 'The Sexual Life of Savages' that didn't make it into Malinowski's book. The anthropologist is supposed to be the disinterested participant observer – he was meant to be close, but not *that* close.

Now the Marxist was talking about Russian money and hotels, Israeli money and hotels, and EU money – not that it existed anymore – and hotels, and the Anthropologist had caught up, he no longer had to fill in the gaps in her monologue retrospectively, he was as they say 'present'. But so was Malinowski. Bloody Malinowski. The VHS had stopped its fast forward and was running in real time, simultaneously, Malinowski in black and white inside the Green Line with the Marxist and the Anthropologist, in the forbidden zone. Terra incognita – no that can't be right, this place has lots of names, too many names, the ability to name confers the ability to control and this place has suffered too much control, terra too much bloody cognita he thought – every blade of shitty grass, every dusty rock, every wheel track monitored and watched over by conscripts in towers and the UN via the remote sensor. Every millimetre, or more likely every tenth of a millimetre, cross referenced, catalogued, mapped, *known*. Too much cross referencing, cataloguing, mapping and knowing in this bizarre city where a journey between the houses of childhood friends a hundred metres apart might be several kilometres long and necessitate two passport checks and a queue. The Marxist had moved on, the Anthropologist was only half listening: casinos, run by the Turkish military, very lucrative or so it was said, vulnerable women from the countryside bussed in and indentured as barmaids and hostesses or worse. In the other half of his mind Malinowski, still in black and white and pith helmet continued to bonk the natives, at least half of his mind impaled on this image, this phrase, of all the others that could come to mind. Couldn't he think about the Kula ring cycle, or conch shells or armlets or something. He tried and again he failed. The images appeared to him out of sync, the Turkish Colonel all flushed and fat, and the atrophied classical anthropologist black and white and grainy. The images mash over each other, they heterodyne, and like white-noise they render each other difficult to read. The Turkish Colonel, fettered by uniform trousers and underpants rumpled around his ankles is, somehow, transposed to the South Pacific Islands? Both the black and white and that odd turquoise colour which characterises 1970s photographs converge, they mesh, and the images start in a bizarre way to make sense; a symmetry, like those old stereoscopic aerial photographs used in the First World War, two 2D flat images are superimposed, and thereby produce one three-dimensional image. The detail is astonishing, a soldier once told the Anthropologist that it was possible to follow a fishing line on a photo taken from ten thousand feet, very nearly two miles up.

The Anthropologist is back, the Marxist has just said 'trouble!' what did she say? He's trying to quickly retrace her steps. Who is in trouble? They are in trouble? He is in trouble? We are in trouble?

It must be that we are in trouble, the flash, that's it, the flash went off and now we are in trouble. 'We are in trouble' she says again. The Anthropologist agrees, he doesn't know why, but it seems the likeliest option, they are in the forbidden zone, standing in the open chatting as if they were in a park in London or somewhere, it's dark of course, that's how they got this far, out the back of her apartment and along by the wire, out into the middle, between the lines, and then the flash went off. Of course, we are in trouble.

**

The soldier was about three metres above their heads. Looking forward, eyes fixed, weapon across his chest, finger hovering over the trigger, squared up, front and centre. It looked as though he had been there for some time.

'We should be ok' said the Marxist, in a voice louder than the Anthropologist would have liked. He wasn't at all sure that they would be ok, but then what did he know? What did she know? The Marxist had no idea of the Anthropologist's background – other than he was born in London, went to school in London, went to college in London, and then back to school again in London. The London School, Malinowski's London school, although that was of course before the Anthropologist's time. The bit in-between, the bit covering his twenties was glossed over, neatly, because his day job covered all eventualities and he was happy to let them be covered. There would be time to elaborate on this with the Marxist, and his Scottish friends would be sure to let the cat out of the bag at some time, but not now, not with a soldier a couple of metres above their head, eyes front and centre, trigger finger hovering. It would confuse the issue, and besides, he was almost a Marxist himself these days.

The Anthropologist considered himself no slouch in getting

away from tricky situations, what with being born in London, and going to school in London, and with what he did in his twenties, but he'd been outclassed tonight. The Marxist was streets ahead of him. He'd kept up physically of course, he runs IronMan triathlons and she was old enough to draw a GLC pension, old enough to remember the GLC in fact, but that was not the point. She was streets ahead intellectually, the first to spot the unmarked police car, the first to even consider the possibility of there being an unmarked police car. The Anthropologist's thoughts had been drifting and without the Marxist he would now be on a hard chair in a bright room trying to explain why he had photographs of the Green Line on his iPhone. It was the Marxist's flash that had gone off, but it would be his phone that they would be going over, the Londoner in dark jeans and a green Gore-Tex jacket. Why this angle, why that sign, why those people? What could he say, that he was writing up a never ending doctorate on nationalism and the construction of identity, south eastern Europe as western Europe's constitutive 'other': oh yes he could say that, and they would listen to him, and then they would write it down in their field notebook, and possibly ask him to write it down in their field notebook too, then they would go away, and when they returned they would ask him what exactly he knew about nationalism and when he said that it was all a pyramid of utter bollocks they would get annoyed, for if the Anthropologist had learned one thing from Belfast to Mogadishu it was that nationalists didn't like to hear that nationalism was a pyramid of utter bollocks. The Anthropologist glanced up at the soldier, still unmoved of course, but that was the sort of chap to whom he would have to explain his ideas about nationalism, and, trigger finger or not, it wouldn't go well.

The Marxist was talking in Turkish. She was fluent in Turkish because she was Turkish, Turkish Cypriot, although as the Anthropologist had learned early on, during that first morning in the fruit market on the Bastion, applying such chauvinist labels was to indulge in a dangerous naiveté. To label is to dominate, and the Marxist wasn't having any of that! She was talking into her mobile phone. They were crouched in the dark under a cactus-like plant behind an electricity substation next to a small roundabout.

The Anthropologist looks again at the soldier above their heads, still unmoved of course, painted black and white on a blood red background. Identical to tens of thousands of mass-produced others, a ribbon-shaped community of motionless grenadiers staring out across northern Nicosia and beyond. YASAK BOLGE GIRILMEZ, Forbidden Zone, Zone Interdite. Did that mean the same thing in Turkish? Forbidden Zone is pretty absolute, unequivocal, no arguing with that, but is it the same in Turkish? How is the forbidden in forbidden zone interpreted, do the sign and the signifier break at the same point, or is it like *sang froid*, impossible to render neatly from one language to the next?

Forbidden Zone. Does it mean that the Greeks are forbidden to enter it, they could at one time and they fucked it up, they persecuted the minority, and the minority – with the help of big cousin – said no, that's forbidden, and so is the area in which we live, to you at least. Forbidden. Or does it mean that the zone itself should be forbidden, an anomaly, an apostate, illegal and unjustified, forbidden by nature, an affront. Forbidden but yet it has to exist, a man-made imposition against the natural order of things. Or does it mean that it's forbidden for anyone to enter it? Yes that's more like it, that's probably what they are getting at, that's why the painted soldier looks so aggressive. When the Marxist is off the phone the Anthropologist will ask her. Well perhaps not straight away, they are still on the run, OTR as they say, and have yet to 'get away with it', they need to concentrate, but it's the sort of question she likes to answer and he likes to pose. Another time. But if that's the case why are all the signs pointed back towards the people they are protecting; the sign doesn't point out at the Other but at the Same, at the Turkish people, and they don't need to be told that it's the forbidden zone, that much is clear from the concrete barrels, the rows of razor wire, the antique sandbags and the thousands of uniformed teenagers looking out on guard. These are all very visible to the people on this side of the wire, and only camouflaged when one looks from the Greek side. People this side wouldn't *want* to go into there. It's a place blighted by atrocity and sterility, surely it would be forbidden?

Yet the Anthropologist knew that they themselves were in there a few minutes ago, plumb in the middle of the forbidden zone, plumb in the middle when the flash went off and all this palaver started. The hushed conversation as if nothing had happened, the blinding searchlight, the megaphoned instructions to walk over to the tower, the Marxist taking the piss out of the policeman behind the megaphone and the conscript behind the searchlight. The Marxist knowing, as if by nature, the rat run through the bushes, the dash through the five-star hotel lobby to make the soldiers think that they were guests and to give them a few metres' breathing space, the fast walk the wrong way round the car park and through the sawgrass and out onto the road. Did Cyprus have snakes? the Anthropologist wondered as they skirted the warm concrete pan of a dark and deserted playground. He assumed so, but then Cyprus is an island and Ireland doesn't have them, and nor does New Zealand. Then a dive through some undergrowth and they ended up here, hiding under this cactus-like bush with the police and the soldiers searching for them and the Marxist on the phone.

Over the Anthropologist's shoulder, shimmering in the last of the heat haze, the spot lamp dots of the Northern Cypriot flag formed and disappeared with a hypnotic regularity. It occurred to him that the only point of its disappearance was for it to reappear

– it was as if the North was being symbolically re-conquered or re-liberated once every twenty-six seconds – not with bombs, but with bling. Denktaş's Disneyland, he once called it, and had been promptly lobbed out of the café in which he sat. But I mean, who else does this, he thought, it's not normal, is it? Perhaps the kindest thing one could say was that it had something of the North Korea about it. He looked up, the Marxist was laughing.

'I'm just asking about his brother's new baby,' she said, covering the mouthpiece of her phone as people once did in the movies. Noticing that the Anthropologist was anxious about the loudness of her conversation she tried to reassure him. He wasn't reassured. Getting away from the flash site, ground zero, that was a good idea, but he didn't see how they could get much further, they were penned in and that too made him anxious. The other side of the wall, on which the sign was hung, bounded a brightly lit dual carriageway, they would be sure to be noticed; and the other way, the way the painted soldier was facing was pitch black and led, from what he could make out, into scrub and wasteland. Snakes or no snakes, he won't be going in there. Hang on ... 'asking whom about his brother's new baby?'

'The taxi firm's night manager,' she said with a wink. 'They love me. They always drop everything to pick me up.'

THE HEART OF NICOSIA

Andriana Ierodiaconou

'Inside the walls, in the heart of Nicosia...' *Tourist Guidebook*
'Archangel Developments – in the green of the country, in the
   heart of the city' *Advertising Billboard, Arkhangeos suburbs of
   Nicosia on an empty tract of future housing development land,
   circa 1979*

In slow suburbs
in fiery lots without tenderness
under stones
in the Archangel's promises
in the green of the banknote and the wish
the heart of Nicosia

In bars at night
THE UNITED NATIONS THE INTERNATIONAL THE
   REGINA
in the Archangel painted to the lips
under Lola, under *Heineken*
on the rocks
the heart of Nicosia

In backstreet shops
under dusty wedding-gowns, light-fixtures, bales of cloth
in the Archangel with tape-measure and scissors
in shop windows, in sentry posts

at the Green Line where we halt
the heart of Nicosia

In kebab stands, in pastry shops
in going home from work at six
under the pure despair and the uniforms
in discos, where the Archangel
dances electric thunderbolts
the heart of Nicosia

In embassies, in consulates
in the Archangel expert diplomat
in neighbourhoods
in churches, mosques, contested areas
under red flags, under blue flags
the heart of Nicosia

EXHIBITION

Nora Nadjarian

Chairs hang from the ceiling. Do not touch. They move themselves, not all the time, not all at the same time. So it's a bizarre effect when a chair, a wardrobe, a bed, seemingly decides to express itself. They hang by invisible wires from the beams and have pencils attached. Their motions write indecipherable messages on blank sheets beneath them: meaningless, desperate, like a memory, or a child's attempt at an alphabet, all over the place. Each one seems to have something to say: the longer you look at it, the more meaningful, the more insistent, the more enigmatic.

The one that spoke to me was the piano stool, the round, wooden, swirling one. I had not seen one of those since the days I used to sit next to my piano teacher, the formidably Russian Miss Nina. A red velvet cushion was placed under my little bottom to make me taller, my small fingers concentrated on Brahms' Waltz in G-sharp Minor and Nina repeated, *More! More open! More open! You are playing closed! You are playing like a cage!*

When she left me to have a pee, always a few minutes before the end of the lesson, I would swirl a full 360 degrees on the stool until she came back. I tried to play "more open" in the last five minutes just to please her, whatever playing open meant. I wanted to play round and round, open and opener, sharper and Majorer, but it all came out sad, flat, G, Flat, Minor.

And the trace made, on the white sheet, is a circle of lines that criss and cross as the stool spins and my little feet swing in and out.

The exhibition space is like a stage. *I would like to thank... I'd like to thank...* And the artist's tongue is tied, she can't remember who. The only person who comes to her mind is her father who used to pack and unpack his suitcase, all on the same day, without travelling anywhere. He would put all his clothes in, and the pipe, and the tobacco. Then he'd lock the suitcase and carry it all the way down the stairs, only to carry it back up again, into the bedroom, onto the bed. And open it. It was a ritual that reminded her that her father was alive, that he was there. She often wanted to slip a message into the suitcase when he wasn't looking: Dad, I love you. Or: You have no idea how much I'll miss you. Or: Please don't go.

The spotlight faces her like a full moon. It blinds her. And they all applaud because her exhibition has reminded them of things about their life that they had long forgotten. The piano stool, the table, the gramophone, the suitcase – all part of the past hanging from the ceiling into the present.

Somebody hugs her. It's her father, dead now for almost four years. He tells her he has read the notes, that it finally now all makes some sense to him. *Thank you,* he says, *I packed my whole life into that suitcase, and there is no longer any need to unpack. I'm home. Finally, I'm home.*

The exhibition space is one street away from The Street of the Whores. The whore is cooking a stew with bay leaves, stirring in other spices from her rack, at random. The front door is open and the place smells divine. Any passer-by would be tempted. Soon, there is a cockroach scratching its legs behind the gas cooker and there is a man sprawled on the sofa, wearing shorts and a stained singlet, and she is saying *I'm coming, I'm coming.* They are a romantic couple, the whore, her client. Even a ménage à trois, if you count the cockroach.

She closes the door and starts taking off her clothes. A big, fat lump of nothing, that's what she knows she is. Her feet almost shuffle as she walks towards him in the dim pink light. She wants to tell him something indecipherable, something meaningless, something desperate about her life. But this is business, and business is business.

The whore's mother insisted on her death bed that she had three daughters, not four. *No, no, the third one died when she was very young, I only have three daughters*, she declared. Her eldest daughter, the one with the perfectly shaped eyebrows, sat on a wobbly chair by her side, held her hand all the time.

A long time ago the whore was a girl. *You can come and kiss me on a first come first served basis*, said the girl with fuchsia breath and she smiled like the bold-coloured flower that she was. She breathed onto their faces, watched them turn pink, red, fuchsia, fire, free.

There is always a beginning, and in the beginning, she sold kisses by the hour. Men came, men went. Gradually, slowly, time passed, life passed, they did strange things to her lips, mouth, nose, ears, hair, skin, turned her body inside out, outside in, smiled, swore, broke her, unbroke her, touched her, undressed her, dressed her, told her stories, bought her, sold her.

She is now a ghost of her former self in the dim pink light. She writes her autobiography in her head. The words are all there, the questions, too. *Tell me, did you once love me? No, I mean really love me. Tell me, did you think of me as a woman or as a whore? Do you still dream of me in fuchsia dreams, the girl I was, the girl I became? If you saw me now in the street, would you recognise me?*

She thinks of the man, sometimes. The man without a name. The man she loved. She loved him, but he insisted on paying her. He loved her, but wouldn't leave his wife for her. Long, long, long ago.

After the exhibition, the restaurant is full of literati and glitterati sipping chilled white wine. Snippets of conversation collide in the air. *Yes – absolutely incredible – I simply – did you? – purest materials – They couldn't possibly have – No, of course not – the raw one ...*

A mobile phone rings. The zip of an enormous handbag opens, zzzzzzzzzip, and then closes again, zzzzzzzzzip, somebody talks to the phone and to the party at the same time, a pregnant woman coughs, a glass of water is knocked over.

It is mid-summer and there is a slight breeze. The candle on the table is blown out, the waiter reappears, apologises, strikes a match, lights the candle, and retires again into the shadow, somewhere to the left of the palm tree. *The baby moved*, the pregnant woman whispers to her husband. *He moved*, she whispers again, and holds his hand.

The morning she finds out she's pregnant, the woman looks at the sky and smiles. It looks almost painted, she thinks. It could have been painted this morning. In nine months' time, she will give birth to a son. He will be the most beautiful creature her eyes have ever seen.

But for now, she admires the sky. It reminds her of a mural she once saw in Florence. She looks for the photo of the mural, but she can't find it. She can never find the photo she wants, in the same way she can never think of the right word to complete a sentence. Instead, in an envelope in one of the drawers of her desk, behind a pile of old letters, she finds five photos. Five photos of her and her husband and a blue sky above their heads. Behind each of the photos, her small, neat handwriting says: Italy, 2005. Behind the sky, she thinks, is a date I had forgotten. On the other side of the sky is a date.

She is not in Italy, but the sky is so blue. The sky is so blue, almost a blessing. Five photos of a blue sky, they lift her spirits. She lays them on the table in front of her, plays around with the order, arranges and re-arranges her own private exhibition. She takes a deep breath, takes in the past, lets it meet her future.

The baby will grow up to become a man. But for now, it is a foetus in the dark. His bones are still soft and pliable, he has not yet been fully formed but his life has started. His mother tells him his life has started, that he will have black hair like his father, that she has given him her green eyes.

There is a sunny spot in the garden, and this is where she stops, like a satisfied tourist, and talks to her unborn son about things he should know about herself and his father. Because we might change, she says, as you grow older. One day we will be different people, we may not even recognise ourselves in the mirror. One day, we may not be able to recognise you. So I want to tell you all this now. I love your father and he loves me. I love you as much as I love the blue, cloudless sky.

The baby moves slightly, it is as slight a movement as the blink of an eye, but enough for her to know that he's listening. *We made you*, she whispers to him, *a long time ago. You were born many years ago, in Italy*.

Days later the artist thinks there is something wrong with her, the way she sees the world all askew, the way she can't balance her feet when she's walking. Like a bird, she can't keep still on the ground. It's almost as if the road she's walking on doesn't exist anymore. But it was here yesterday, she mutters, to no one but herself. But I was here yesterday. Step by step, she thinks she is escaping reality. Her life is a figment of her imagination, playing tricks on her mind. Whenever she passes by a mirror, she smoothes the worry lines, she smiles, tries to remember her face when it was younger.

On difficult, unbalanced days, she photographs graffiti or takes found objects home and polishes them like there's no tomorrow. Once she found a pebble. A pin. Part of a sponge, a shell, a broken light bulb, a shoelace, a receipt. She wanted to record the sound a pebble might make under her foot as it clicks against another. She wanted to make an asymmetrical sculpture, one that would inspire longing in people. The feeling of longing, the sensation that only those who have lost something would know about. *Excuse me, have you lost something?*

She wonders how long the road is back to her childhood. *But you can't go back*, said her father, *only forward*. Yet she longs for something. *For what?* asks her father. *I just long for*, she replies. *It's a state of being, longing for. Something.*

The bird lands, and hops. She feels that she is hopping from one place to another in the same city, like a homeless person, a nestless bird. Her father visits her in dreams and tells her: *You're making an exhibition of yourself.* She wants to make sculptures out of things people have lost. *I've lost a pin, a pebble, a coin, an eyelash, my heart, my mind. What are you longing for? What have you lost? When did you last see your heart? Did you pack the suitcase yourself? Please do not leave baggage unattended.* People always want an answer to make them feel good, she thinks. And she knows that when there is no reply to a question, it is considered an asymmetry.

She thinks of her mother. They went to church every Sunday, she lit candles. But her mother was discovered one afternoon, when her husband came home early from work, went up the stairs and opened the door. The whole neighbourhood held its breath. So you've been married to a whore all these years, they didn't ask. So your daughter might not even be your own, so nothing you know is true, so somebody pulls a carpet from under your feet, and you lose your balance. Look out, you're about to fall. And her father lost everything he thought he had, securely, in his hands, his head, his past, his present. Start packing, follow her, change your mind, unpack. You're a loser, a fucking loser, whose wife walked down some stairs and disappeared from his life. He sometimes wishes he'd come home early that night only to find that the lock on the door had been changed. Then everything would have been different. Then nothing would have happened.

The city hides its secrets. If you want to explore, walk in and out of the present, into the past, way back into the past, follow narrow paths and open doors to re-enter the present, to go round cement blocks, in and out of artificial lights.

I, the author of this story, am putting things in the right order or no order at all. I am trying to express in words how I was never able to play the piano openly. My playing was rigid, cemented. Nowadays I prefer to listen to CDs, and write. I am opening up in other ways, I suppose. I've found the key of the cage. I've discovered some words and I'm putting them together and I'm writing and writing.

The exhibition of the hanging chairs is still on. I went to see it again yesterday. There they were, all the seemingly random objects on seemingly random display, hanging from the ceiling. The whore's chair, the artist's father's suitcase, her mother's bed, Miss Nina's piano stool. I stood in the middle of it all, and I didn't know how long I spent listening to their stories, to the silence charged with their unearthly frequency.

Tonight there is a gecko on the wall, a tiny creature with tiny black eyes like beads, a transparent body. I want to keep it there for company, on my wall, forever, to illuminate it with a coloured light. But it moves away, runs away from me, hides somewhere in the dark.

Miss Nina plays a Nocturne by Chopin. I try to catch the music in my hands, I pretend to be playing it myself beautifully, faultlessly. I am seven years old. For once, Miss Nina does not speak. For once, I long for her to tell me off, to tell me I'm playing it all wrong. I long for her irritated voice, her Russian accent. But she says nothing at all. She turns the pages of the book and plays another Nocturne and then another. I swirl 360 degrees on the stool next to her and finally I lose her, she's gone. All I have is the music in my head. C. Sharp. Minor. There is no book, no piano, no room.

Things shift from here to there and from there to here. The ghosts of the old town write their diaries. Please don't touch the exhibits, they move on their own.

RED LEFKOŞA DREAMS

Constantia Soteriou

To Stavros

Every night you have the same dream. At 3 o'clock in the morning; that you are becoming a woman. Every night you dream of becoming a woman.

In your dreams you went to Arif's funeral, you dressed in black, you wore the black scarf, you covered your hair, in your dreams, it was a dream, a dream, dream, dream, you crossed the barricades, you ran in the old city, you ran wearing the black high heels he loved, taka-taka-taka at the cobbled street, taka-taka-taka. You, running in the cobbled street thinking of him, becoming beautiful for him, becoming beautiful to go to his funeral, to go to the mosque to see him, to honour him. Wearing black, covering your hair, becoming beautiful just to see him.

They did not let you in, they did not let you see him. They pushed you back out of the mosque. You heard the imam chant for him, you saw the green prayers rising, you saw them looking at you, staring at you. What is this Rum woman doing here? What is this beauty doing here, here at the Turkish side, here, and you, pretending that you do not understand, pretending that you do not hear, pretending that this is not you, you went there in your dream, you dreamt that you went to his funeral, you went to his funeral dressed as a woman, in your dream, you went as a woman, you coward, you crook, you bastard, you dreamt that you were at his funeral, you went there only in your dream.

Every night you have the same dream. At 3 o'clock in the morning; that you are becoming a woman. Every night you dream of becoming a woman. Every night at 3 o'clock in the morning you are a woman.

Your eldest nanny, the great great grandmother, was the *dünya-güzeli*, the most beautiful woman in the whole world. They called her Fairy. She was loved by a man called Hasan. He went to find her, to take her, 'I will take her', he said, 'I will take you, you will become mine'. She did not want to, she did not want to go, she could not change who she was.

'Listen', she said, 'let them fight! Your Allah and my Christ. Let them fight. Let's see who will win. So you can have me. So you can lose me. Let them fight.' This is what she said.

They fought for days, her Christ and his Allah, they fought for months and years. The Christ got tired, he was about to lose the battle. The Fairy got scared, Hasan got sad. The gods felt bad, the gods felt miserable. 'Give hands', Hasan said. 'Give hands'. The gods gave hands. Hasan became a Christian. But he promised Allah to give him a piece of his penis to God. He promised to give a piece of every male son to Allah. This is why they circumcise all the males in your family. You gave a piece of your penis to Allah. This is how the story happened, this is what the great great grandmother said, this is what the Fairy asked. This is how the gods won.

You decided not to sleep, ever, at nights. Never. Again.

'You need an onion, you cut it in small pieces, you fry it a bit, you wait. You take two red tomatoes, you put in the pan, you stir, you wait. You put your bulgur, you stir, you put the water, you stir, you wait. You put it away from the fire, you put your salt, you say the spell, you spit, you stir, you wait. You wait. You cover the pan with a red scarf. It has to be red. A red scarf. You wait. You have to wait. Wait. Serve him, say the spell, say the magic words, tell the god, ask the god, make him love me. Make him love me. Make him love me. He will love you. He will love you. He will love you.'

A tried and trusted recipe Emine Abla gave your aunt Maria. You are doing something wrong. You are missing some ingredients. Nobody loved you. Ever.

Every night you have the same dream. At 3 o'clock in the morning; that you are becoming a woman. Every night you dream of becoming a woman. You feel it while sleeping, you are changing, you are becoming her, your hands are thinner, your nails are red, hairs are growing in your head, your breasts are pulsing. You are emasculating. Every night, at 3 o'clock in the morning; every single night at three in the morning. This is how you dream. This is your Lefkoşa dream. This is a coward's dream at 3 o'clock in the morning.

TO BASTEJKALNA PARK

Jenan Selçuk

Translated by Aydın Mehmet Ali

Without a doubt, this is a magical garden
  Those escaping their roots
Turn into fairies with palm-sized buttocks

The eyes search for cameras, there must be a photo-shoot
Perhaps a celebration, no, not possible, you can't convince me
        That today is just another day

Even the park-keepers are women in this park,
        or is it no entry for men?
Just as you begin to say there is nothing more perfect
Nature slaps you in the face, you are wrong; there is always *better*
    than the *better*
Hey Pushkin's statue I confess I envy you

I shrink back even further on this bench I've merged with
Of course I don't mind, if you sit next to me.
  It's so obvious, isn't it? I'm not from around here ...

Tell me, how do I walk the back-streets of the Walled City
How do I stop myself from spitting
        into the faces of those who spit everywhere
Tell me you pimps, on my return to Cyprus, how can I walk again
    On those putrid pavements that darken the human soul?

GARDENING DESIRE

Stavros Stavrou Karayanni

Ali Ejaz hummed tunes familiar from Bollywood. His handsome voice was hesitant, tentative, but intent on making itself heard in the darkling spring air of Nicosia's Parliament Park. The evening breeze carried his song across the parterres, over the hedges, brushed it along the thorny edges of the cactus shoots, and lifted it all the way through the rich rustling foliage of the giant eucalyptus. As dusk began to descend, the shadows in the park multiplied, offering refuge to anxious promises. I approached, fully in love with the idea of his dark complexion against the settling evening, and traced the lines of his face enquiringly and longingly, happily settling on eyes, bright with a smile that rested within the lines on the sides and on his mouth – full lips and always ready for a smile. These encounters, at once magical and devastating; not knowing what to relish foremost, the pungent flesh, the skin that mixes strong aftershave with cigarette smoke – a scent that to me breathes the most concentrated excess of sexual longing. On our way through the park and out of the gate, the euphoria from my fulfilment evoked a desire in me to offer something from another dimension, I wanted to give him something as a token of how I loved him at that moment, but all I had to give was my name, as if this could be an offering, a humble gift of sorts. 'Ali Ejaz,' he replied.

The Nicosia Municipal Gardens is a serene and pleasant park, the legacy of British colonial rule. For more than a century it has existed across from the Nicosia General Hospital (now demolished) just outside the city's sixteenth-century Venetian wall, its east side facing the Paphos Gate. The Parliament building, on the south side, adorns the colonial legacy with the premises of the esteemed and venerable legislative body of the Republic of Cyprus, and assigns its label: Parliament Park. Its other names, however, are much more alluring and even offer a tour of the political history of Cyprus: the British called it, rather surprisingly, Victoria Memorial Gardens. More recently, Asian migrants, whose personal histories are inherently connected with the same colonial narrative, refer to it as Cyta Park (the Cyprus Telecommunications Authority being the biggest telecommunication company active in the island), a name that acknowledges the island's corporate accomplishments gone awry in March 2013 when Laiki Bank, one of the Republic's biggest banks, collapsed. And, in light of the developments of the last few years, Garden of Peace is the name that marks the ever so slight shifts in the nationalist narratives that have ensured that the island's wounds are kept open.

Yet, the most appealing name is one that I remember in my childhood and that associates the park with its benefactor, Princess Zena Gunther de Tyras, whose financial support, along with the architectural plans of Neoptolemos Michaelides, engendered the landscaping that we have inherited today, even though its appearance must be quite different from the early 60s when Michaelides set about re-designing it. What an extraordinary stroke of camp fortune that this park would be associated with a princess whose life story reveals a bruised femininity that is so appealing to men conscious of their compromised masculinity. Zena Gunther, a Tala-born girl, in the province of Paphos, and a Limassol cabaret dancer who married the heir of the Gunther family and came into extraordinary wealth, in order to, among many other things, restore a park, give it her name and establish a meeting point for men who engage in an active negotiation with the norms of masculine behaviour and masculine power, and, more importantly, the uses of pleasure on the landscape of the male body made possible by the landscape of the garden.

I used to visit this park when I was a little boy. Yet, memory works in striking ways. It is not merely a passive repository but an active catalyst building experience, shaping the imaginative land-scape that processes our lives. I still remember the feeling of going to this park to admire the aviary (I loved animals, birds, serpents and always sought opportunities for contact), but an even greater impression was created by those men who walked around the park or sat on the benches looking forlorn but insistently present and queerly purposeful. I looked with curiosity and fascination as if I could fathom their extraordinary purpose despite my young age and lack of sexual experience.

How much of what we remember is actual memory and how much is projection of subsequent thoughts and experiences mod-elled on vague recollections without solid references? Did I really know what those men looked for in the park or did I apply this knowledge in retrospect? Whatever the case, years later when I found myself an adult sitting on those benches observing in wait, my imaginative point of reference became those male figures that traversed the late morning shadows of my childhood, the present experience constructed on those shadowy foundations. My heart beat in my mouth that first time I cruised in this park of Nicosia. I was seventeen, insecure and unknowing but persistent and inquis-itive, and I relished with great guilt, shame, but also elation the bizarre pleasure as the electric charge of sex surged in my youth-ful body. As if in supplication, the unknown man, who was much older than I was at the time, knelt before me with tenderness and appreciation. I think back on that first experience with great fondness even though it really wasn't much in terms of sexual adventure. Rather, it was an unceremonious initiation to the mysteries of cruising, but sufficient for me to taste pleasure and sense the intoxication of a proscribed exchange whose contours I had already traced in the mysterious area that lies beyond the known frames of verbal reference.

'Where should we go?' he whispered as we walked away from the bench where he had been sitting surveying the desiring human traffic as it shadowed its way through the park.

'Well', I replied, 'the choices are rather limited: there is Hedge A on our right, Hedge B on our left, a shrub further up, and the dark parking lot across the street.' Decisions are taken quickly at these moments and soon we were both headed towards my car parked in the dark parking lot across the street from the Parliament Park. Once inside he wasted no time lowering the seat and lying back in a relaxed position offering himself in a way that was attractive and inviting, unlike the typical macho attitude that determines the motion of such poses, favourite with straight-identified men who expect to be 'serviced' slavishly. On our initial exchange I felt a certain sweetness about him. He had a rare disposition of knowing what he wanted and the confidence to request it in a manner that incited my desire. Yes, apart from his appealing looks, it was the way he composed our love encounter that charmed me. I was so taken by the wonderful way he offered himself and was quite shocked that he lingered for a short while after so as to share a little about himself. When we parted, I walked away thinking about how this man came along to love me on this dark, cool October night, add texture to my life and leave me with a lingering taste of desire in my mouth. Reaching the traffic lights of Strovolos Avenue, I observed as if in a trance, the lights of cars gliding up and down the busy crossroads staring with their bright and unwavering intentness. My mouth felt those pathways crafted by his presence, sadly tracing the absence. And I caressed the seat beside me and brought my hand to my nose several times, like the stray cat that frequents my mother's backyard and who comes and sniffs my car tyres deciphering with intentness smells that registered and travelled on that spot. His strong body smell is, in fact, what I found most overpowering. What is it about a lover's smell that lingers in your nostrils and you inhale it like a precious narcotic relishing it as if it will induce that state of ecstasy again or make the sensation of that body recur? And the cars kept gliding around me in all directions it seemed – as if each one of them was carrying him but forbidding me to have him, goading me as this insufferable absence enveloped me.

There are many remarkable things to observe about cruising encounters, however furtive, secretive and evanescent they may be. Almost every time, despite the darkness and sometimes even the wordless character of the exchange, important attributes may become apparent. Proximity is enough to offer some intimation of the world that the stranger's body inhabits and to bespeak compatibility or otherwise. All it takes is a shadow, a hurried or languid movement in the dark, a pause and a process. And what you perceive often allows your imagination to take you on these journeys that awaken secret desires and evoke that hunger for sensation. As if caught unaware, even though it is there for the purpose, the body rises to the pleasure of looking and welcomes the surge of emotive synaesthesia.

At present the cruising scene in Nicosia has seen further developments. Since April 2003 the line of separation between

North and South has opened, allowing people to travel between the two parts of the island for the first time in twenty-nine years. Inevitably, some of the Greek Cypriots began to cruise in Northern Cyprus, and Turkish Cypriots ventured to the parks and parking lots in the south. Meetings and sexual encounters between gay men of the two communities have seen the materialization of what used to be an old fantasy of compromising contact between the infidel and the religiously devout; the insolent and the refined. Dissident desire (gay, lesbian and so much more) often wants to transcend the oppressive boundaries of dominant narratives, and shows greater willingness to cross borders and defy prejudice. Yet, dissidence does not always presume innocence and lack of prejudice. The manner in which a Greek Cypriot man will approach a Turkish Cypriot man for sex during cruising will be in negotiation with nationalist indoctrination and the long and systematic cultivation of hatred.

Apart from Turkish Cypriots, Nicosia cruising has seen the appearance of immigrants looking for sex for pleasure and/or money. In the eighties, the only non-Greek Cypriot one might see would be Lebanese fleeing from the civil war. Now there are ethnic Greeks from the Black Sea region, African asylum seekers, South Asian migrant workers, Western Europeans working in off-shore companies, and men from Eastern Europe. Without access to internet chat lines and because cruising in person is the only way to find other men, these men have re-introduced into cruising some of the pulse that was usurped by on-line meeting sites.

The park with many names, just on the outskirts of the Venetian walls of a city torn apart by violence, occasions reflections on colonial and postcolonial historical moments, migration, global sexual developments and shifts in sexual attitudes in Cypriot society. The vegetation itself has suffered greatly in recent years. A systematic effort to eliminate all possible hiding places – every corner where something or anything could be concealed – has left the park bereft of hedges, bushes, climbers. The trees have grown much taller but the park has never looked so bare. And the behaviour has also seen shifts. Patriarchy, with its dependence on easily recognisable sexual roles that will attempt to perpetuate set power systems, has established the dichotomy of effeminate and passive on the one hand and macho and active on the other. Nevertheless, this dichotomy has slowly been subsumed into more complex pursuits of pleasure and negotiations of masculinity, thus changing considerably the behaviour of cruising men in an unforgiving and relentlessly 'straight' society. And heartbeats continue to punctuate the humid darkness, as Nicosia changes into its park gear for pleasure pursuits.

Moving through the shadows, a glorious moon overhead as if it's the only place where it shines its full light – the rest of the planet is completely deprived of its silver overtones, smooth and mellow bathing the landscape, playing with it as if to drive everyone and everything mad with transcendence. The corridor of tall palm trees, the sharpness of the breeze, the silhouettes of the cacti stretching upwards in the darkness and a man, tall, heavy, dressed in jeans, is walking from the opposite direction. He slows down, and as soon as he passes me he stops and I look back and he does too, and before long we are in the tenuous safety of the park's hedges. In the shadowy light our texts of desire become very legible and we begin to read them to each other, tentatively and haltingly at first. Steadily, however, the reading gains in devotion and tenor. Soon we begin to apply our lips to words, to whole sentences, and we traverse the textual passages hungrily, passionately. We take each other's words and turn them around in our mouths, tasting their every edge, tracing their pulse, their heat, their texture. There is no stopping this articulation; so full of ardour, so adroit, and happening against the backdrop of his smell: it reminded me of my aunt's courtyard in her old, now demolished house where I used to play with my cousins in a childhood of smells that blended wet earth, oleander, basil and bay leaf, bitter and sweet and pungent. And when we finished our passages, we put our texts away and parted, feigning a certain nonchalance about the anxious moment of saying goodnight. And I walk on through the bushes, up the path, through the side entrance, across the empty street and finally onto busy Egypt Avenue, my head immersed in the effort to control the flow of what I still can't identify but which I know flows from a certain point on the landscape of my memory, as if his desire reached out and stroked that point and probed it until this energy burst forth and danced around me, ineluctable, wounding, and un-regenerate.

GHOST WHISPERS AT THE ARMENIAN CEMETERY, NICOSIA

Lisa Majaj

I remember the day I died. Heat glazed the sky, its pale tinge reflecting off the heat-struck stones of the walls that hold the city, that encircle and confine it within a past that has been written a thousand times, that cries out to be rewritten. The priest's voice rose in the chapel, mingled with the cries of my mother who tore at her hair in grief. Those who went before keep me company here in this place of stone and memory, cypress trees gray with summer dust, ashen from everything they have seen. What I have seen is buried now, like my eyes – but I didn't disappear, although the earth swallowed me. Bones make their claim even if they are disinterred; they stay like a testament. Under each marble headstone, listen: stories are stirring. Here is the taste of the communion wafer of my childhood, the priest with his long beard pulling my ear when I whispered in church. Here is the old lady at the bakery, smiling as she slipped me sweet buns. Here is the smell of coffee from the coffee shop, the click of dice on the *tawleh* board. I remember the bell in the chapel: I can still hear its chime, like an old man singing. When my sight failed me as I lay on my deathbed, I listened for that bell to link me, flesh to stone to earth. I didn't hate anyone in my life. Why should I choke on dust? This city was built inside me echo by echo, memories tactile as dirt in my hand. It's up to you, now, to listen to the stories the city tattooed on my bones. The day my mother washed my body with cool water and closed my eyes with a trembling hand, I became a stone in the wall of this city – and grew roots and tendrils.

MY NAME IS QUEER

Despina Michaelidou

weird ...
subversive ... abnormal ...?

I cross sides divisions and the order of things

If I were a colour I could be black maybe white...
or all the colours of the rainbow, shining glittery...

Who am I? Who are you? Who are we? Who is the Other?
In between death and life

    I am here waiting for you
You are here waiting for me

Can you see me? Touch me?
Can you feel me? Smell me?

I am not a woman and neither are you a man
You are not a woman and I am not a man
I don't even know if we are human

Here we are
The Other and the I the I and the Other
We look into the mirror
You think you recognize me I think I recognize you

I can see you and touch you
I can feel you. Or do I ...?

We, the thousand pieces of a broken and colonized mirror
Borders and binaries of you and me the Other and the I

Imprisoned segments of trapped identities bodies masks norms ...
Does it matter if we are young old thin fat able-bodied ... or not

What if we are gay bi lesbian straight transgender cisgender
single with or without children (a)sexual polyamorous monoga-
    mous

How about nationalism? Are we patriots?
capitalists socialists anarchists?

We are questioning patriarchy feminism right and left
our truths lies freedoms occupations friends enemies

Our name is queer
We are nothing and everything; traitors to the nation

Where is home?
Lefkoşa Λευκωσία Nicosia

Home reconnects the I and the Other
Scents of jasmine cinnamon lemon blossoms and songs of violin
    oud *pithkiavli*
Feeling my way through transcendental bodies and senses

I look again into the mirror
I am sorry I say to the I and the Other for the scars of the past

I run naked towards the unknown unapologetic

I feel broken fixed fearless hopeless
I attempt to recreate our shared times places truths lies

My name is queer
Mourning without tears
for herstory
But what about our... future?

THE PHOTO – THE GUARD POST

Haji Mike

The politicians, huh ... they'll be on the dole when Cyprus becomes One. Beyond that lies what? The Unknown ... unless of course you believed everything you saw and heard on the tell-lie-vision. The north of Cyprus became like a bird sanctuary. You could not go to it but you could look through binoculars for a fee way up high in the Shacolas building in the middle of Ledra Street in the early 1990s. Going there a few times, as a taboo tourist, zooming in mainly on the flag on the hill in a vain hope of spotting the village beyond all the concrete that had sprouted so profusely on both sides of the green line in Nicosia. Of course the village was never sighted.

Around 1992 he became famous overnight as a 'singer'. 'I never wanted to be a star', Cat Stevens once declared on the last LP he made, 'Izitso', before becoming Yusuf Islam, and this musician felt the same way. Fame was irrelevant. Some fortune would be nice, to make up for all those years lugging speakers around venues, but the celebrity status was futile, particularly when all the glossy magazines were full of tacky shots of people posing. Reminding him of a line from 'Plastic People': 'even if you're out of tune, it can be fixed, even with a snip, eliminate the glitch.'

It had become clear to him that in Cyprus 'you are what you declare'. In the photos stood people wearing designer clothes, fake couples and fake smiles, painfully fake smiles. A commentator in a weekly rag called these types 'zopovortoi' which does not translate very well into English. How do we say it, 'vortos,' a person who could not care less about anything, and 'zopos' an idiot/a clown. He added the epithet 'nouveau' zopovortoi – a mashup post-modernist version being zopovortex – in the mix. These were the nouveau riche Nicosia types (although a Limassolian and on rare occasions Ayia Napatin could also be sighted). They just loved to be seen week in, week out. It was a case of going to these tacky events to be seen so the photographers could snap away and put you in the magazines. To be seen so they could say they saw you. Long before photo apps re-invented grids on mobiles these mags had them by the lorry load, page upon page of people posing with painfully fake plastic smiles. Many of the people posing were also media types, people in radio who had declared themselves to be 'producers', and yet they knew nothing about actually producing music. People in business who maybe owned a clothes store or two. And the politicians, oh, the politicians with their limited tunnel visions. Most of these folks had largely declared the singer a persona non grata because he dared to use a few Cypriot words in his songs. He was to them a flash in the pan, going against the grain of fake pop Greekness. And truth be told to them, and himself but for completely different reasons, he was not really a singer, he was more of an MC but they never got that. 'What happened to you?' asked an aging TV producer on the state TV channel, 'Why do you sing so fast – did you swallow the transistor radio?' It does sound much better in the vernacular: 'ekatapies to transistor mana mou?' So, to many he was a 'singer', even though he was a poet/MC.

When the magazine approached him, one of those glossy ones, full of the aforementioned zopovortex types, he decided, inspired by the Punk Rock spirit of 1977 (which by the way hardly anyone at the time in Cyprus knew), to be photographed in a way that defied the order of things. He also selected the photographer, a documentary maker friend, who perhaps knew what Punk Rock was. 'I want to take some photos in noman's land' he declared to his friends, one of whom was the photographer, at a gathering of musicians and artists in a house right next to the green line. A guard post actually stood nearby. It was a strange place to be at night, not really knowing what might happen if you took a wrong step.

'It can be done', said the photographer. 'But it depends where you want to take the pictures'.

'Ledra Palace, no man's land' he declared feeling the rebellion in his words amongst some of the people there. Some looked a bit shocked. Others uninterested. There was a hint of *katexomenisation* in some of their eyes though. Anything beyond a certain point was *katexomena* – 'occupied' – and you could not step any further because it was taboo. And making this into a dogma, a doctrine led to all kinds of anomalous reactions. For example, Theodorakis was declared a traitor by some for playing with Livaneli in Turkey, despite the fact that they sang for peace. 'I would boycott anything to do with them', another singer urged (he was a 'patriot'). He had attended a protest event the following Friday where a handful of poets were coming together in peace as Cypriots. One of the poets he had met as a teenager at a student gathering in London. In fact he was allocated the task of translating for her. The poet had raised a simple question. 'My country is divided in two. Which part should I love?' How could anyone advocate boycotting questions from Cypriots?

Ah, you said that word again in the plural. It was a word that was shunned in the early 1990s. Cypriots. There, you said it again. Don't say it too often. The patriots on this trip kept correcting him time and time again. 'We Are Greeks', but somehow he never fell for it. One teacher a few months before sat on a TV chat show on the state broadcaster and declared he was Cypriot and not Greek, and the next day the Unions went on strike. They declared that if the show was repeated (as so often happened) they would down their tools. Strange Unions they have back in the homeland, he thought. Where was the problem, the singer wondered? A teacher just said what so many people had felt all their lives. Ask those Greek school teachers about how they pulled our ears in the late 60s when we said 'tzai' in north London! The same TV station also banned an interview with Theodorakis and of course imposed an informal ban on all things Yusuf/Cat Stevens. The teacher was also slammed in the glossy mags and patriotic press. They called him a 'Neo-Cypriot' and even a 'paedophile'. The second accusation totally inaccurate and slanderous. The first a strange concoction, really, as there was hardly anything 'neo' about being Cypriot. We were as ancient as the Phoenicians. And yet ...

'It can be done,' said the photographer. 'It's just a process and I will look into it'.

Just wanna be free to walk across the land, from town to town without a passport in my hand
Just wanna be free to go from place to place without the barrel of a gun in my face

In between the gigs, radio shows, late nights and talking till the sun came up, he also developed a strong liking for carrot juice. Freshly made and drunk at 5am after the gigs. It was the natural alternative to energy drinks, which so many musicians and DJs got addicted to. Shark at 5am, keeps you awake till 5pm the next day. 'It's not easy what you are asking for', declared a wise cousin contemplating late one night while sucking his straw on carrot. 'Taking pictures in the dead zone is risky.' Slurrrp-slurrp. 'There's a lot of paperwork. First of all you would have to approach the relevant office in our government. Then they would have to contact the United Nations, who then I assume would have to discuss it with the Occupying Army.' As a procedure it all seemed so futile. After all, it was just some photos. The no man's land, the dead zone, the buffer zone, conjured up so many thoughts. You could not go one step beyond a certain point. But he wanted to take so many steps beyond towards his village, in freedom, where peace would reign supreme, with no soldiers, tanks or guns or bullets or presidential decrees declaring who was a traitor and who was a 'this' and 'that'. Things could be so polarised sometimes in Cyprus – so fanaticised and fixed. Just like that memory down a dusty road in Famagusta in 1968 when certain kids refused to play with other kids because 'they' were 'right' and 'we' are 'left' – so know your left from your right, he was told coldly, and don't play with them. But the only us and them he knew was Tottenham and Arsenal, and yet he still talked to his older brother. *Left wing right wing chicken wing plane wing every kind of wing ting is the same sing ting.*

The call came from the photographer on the phone. He was happy. The permission was granted. They could go to Ledra Palace for the shoot. So early one morning he put on his matching Ragga-like cord jacket and trousers and a cloth woven baseball cap and headed to a place he had never been before. 'When these walls come down in our minds, and only then, will they come down in real life', a wise sister had once told him back in Dalston, London. That statement always stayed in his mind. Just like the one made by an ageing South African artist he once met who had lived in a Commune in Paris in 1968. 'Whatever happens, always keep the flame alive and just pass it on'.

The phrases walked with him on that morning. He rewound them back and forward trying to comprehend a future without walls and lines that divide. It was fairly straightforward. We don't want war! A piece of paper was handed over to the soldier who asked a couple of questions. He was a 'blue-skull', a UN peacekeeper. He stressed no photos could be taken in areas where they were 'prohibited'. It did sound like a tall order for a couple of people about to embark on a photo shoot in no man's land, but what he was trying to say was no photos of military personnel, guard posts, and no pointing telephoto lenses in a way that might be deemed 'provocative'. It was a strange feeling being in this space. There were no cars. Hardly any sounds. Just our feet on the ground walking to a couple of old derelict buildings, which would later become an upmarket bar function spot where Nicosia-ites, diplomats and significant dignitaries would wine and dine in the buffer zone. Well, that was twenty years on, when the checkpoints opened and for a few days a whole sea of people wanted to go and see the lands beyond. That was some trip, but it's really another story.

The graffiti amazed him more than anything. It was crazy how anyone could sneak in here and spray all kinds of things on the walls, from 'I love you' to girlfriends and homage to football teams to a call for 'Union with Greece' – 'Enosis' – a faded dream which in reality had brought us all to this much-divided spot in the heart of Nicosia. There was a wall with a crude attempt at doing a protest mural and beyond that the 'other' side existed just like any other street, but across the distance of the dry, barren football pitch. Taking all this in, the photographer snapped away. He liked natural shots, which was more comfortable on the singer because he had had enough of fake smiles this year, posing for magazine covers, newspapers and celebrity gossip columns. It was a cold place – it lacked emotion – but it was also a frozen place. He had been warned about this kind of view because division had an essence, there always had to be someone to blame. 'Don't forget, always remember' – *'den sxechno'* – that worn-out cliché term that a whole generation had been weaned on. He also noticed it on one of the walls of the abandoned building. Worn out, faded but still there waiting to be read. 'It's an issue of invasion and occupation', he had been told religiously time and time again. All refugees to their homes. All 'settlers' back to Turkey and every single millimetre of the '*katexomena*' occupied lands – back to their rightful owners. Does that also include Turkish Cypriots, he always asked. After all, they lost their homes too. His aunt would always tell him to 'ssshhh' when asking such questions, because people had died for asking them before. But all the stale talk sounded so good to the Greek Cypriot ear, and every school book this side of 1974 had the slogan emblazoned on each cover and he did not like stale talk. So many politicians had come and gone. A whole generation of dead people exiled from their homes, and the slogans still remained, just like the 'problem' unsolved. But some of the questions he asked when he would not 'ssshhh' made one bunch of raving right-wing looneys in London declare they would 'kneecap' him 'IRA style', along with other people, such as the recent President, and a few other peace-minded folks, who they had declared as 'traitors' and 'antihellines' (anti-christ/anti-Greeks).

'So where are the actual guard posts?' he asked the photographer. 'Well we can't go inside them here, because here it's more complicated, not possible, but we can go somewhere else I know.' As they prepared to leave Ledra Palace some of the 'Blue Skulls' were all smiles, exhibiting a kind of informed naiveté. They were just doing their job keeping the peace – it felt like a bit of a holiday camp for them compared to wars raging in Somalia, Georgia and the uprising in Iraq (which they had not quite stepped into back then). The photographer held his camera waist-level and clicked away contented at bullet-ridden buildings. Whole chunks taken out of Ledra Palace rocked the singer visually. 'That was from the fighting in 1974. The holes still exist to this day, as does the green line'.

Weaving through the narrow streets, a few songs came to mind.

'Oliver's Army' apparently has a line in it about 'murder mile'. Elvis Costello wrote it on a plane back from Belfast at the height of 'the Troubles'. It could have been any narrow road parallel to Ledra Street in the late 1950s. Bob Marley's 'One Love' conjured up an image of a Rasta man sitting in no man's land playing a binghi drum chanting down Babylon. His mind wandered into a surreal scenario. He had disappeared mysteriously in 1981, and just like Tupac he was not selling incense sticks down Ridley Road Market in Dalston.

'What is all this?' he quizzed Bob, looking round at the dry, barren football stadium surrounded by guns. Bob replied, 'Let's get together to fight this holy Armageddeon'. Then some voices just floated, soulful, heavenly harmonies, Sweet Harmony in the Rock stood on the old Venetian Walls separating the two sides of the city rocking slowly in unison singing 'We shall overcome', casting long, solemn, dramatic shadows. Amidst all these, Billy Liar daydreams of peace. They zoomed through the streets heading to a place east of the city centre. It was an industrial estate that ran parallel with the green line. Must have been Kaimakli. The photographer told him to stay by the car for a moment, as he had to seek out a friend who might be able to get them in the guard post.

It was as small as a toilet. The solider who showed them around looked nervous and excited, and couldn't have been older than eighteen. The singer tried to relax his nerves by autographing a photo. They exchanged small talk on what team they were 'with'. Just then a loud howl from a neighbour broke the late morning peace like a lion roaring in the still of night with a toothache. 'What's a civilian doing in a military guard post?' he shouted, and shouted louder and louder three times over. Being on the green line, a few metres from the other side, he suddenly felt that threat, that uncertainty, that death vibe. The three of them froze, momentarily like statues. A spilt second past and the photographer, who had been clicking away, suddenly stopped and declared 'Mate, we have to go ...' They shot out avoiding the neighbour, who was till howling. Sweet Honey, Bob and Elvis Costello all rewound through his mind like a mash-up mix gone wrong. The young solider had another twenty-two months to go on his national service. The most pointless experiences of his life before him dressed in 'the green'. The singer hoped the incident would not make the youth serve an extra couple of months as punishment for bending the rules. The *filakeio* (guard post) disappeared in the distance of the rear-view mirror and looking ahead everything raced through his mind like the future going backwards. This was the history of now. A few days later the photographer brought him the contact prints. He started to go over them with a highlighter, suggesting a few shots he liked. From the photos in the guard post, one of them caught the distress of that moment, frozen in time. He called that one the 'complain neighbour' shot. The photos came out a couple of weeks later, when he was back in his London bedsit above Trehantiri Music Store, where the trains rocked his bed noisily from side to side as they went over the nearby bridge. You get used to it after a few nights. Here on Green Lanes the only green line that separated people was a construct of frustrated minds. He showed the article to a few friends. 'We also went into a guard post – those photos did not make the article' he said.

DARKROOM DELAY

Dinda Fass

Shadows cross nothing street

Watched across minutes
a soldier slowly appears
is gone

Crossing point reflecting a riddle:
Each day a map stops

Day unfolds, irrespective,
paces the maze

Yet distance makes the story remote
strange erasion of skywashed identities.

CALLIOPE

Dinda Fass

Walking a deserted edge

Come to broken growing up
See me fear a gun
I walk in front, he walks behind.

One day I don't see the thing itself
Look! Mystery cracks open

Voices, girls, shoes
the world book drones on
A continuous line of imaginations, of propagandas.

Turn to the green beginning,
Blink

ALIF ... BAA ... TAA ...

Bahir Laattoe

For Aydın and Shereen

Alif
The setting. Rüstem Bookshop. Dating from 1937. So long before 1974. First thought: I want to live here. But John Wyndham, Spike Milligan, Solzhenetsin, Atatürk, *The History of Turkey in Cyprus, We are all Americans Now* (or something like that), *The Secrets of Home Freezing*, all live here. Cheek by jowl. This bookshop was a house once. The bookshop was on the ground floor then, and the family were on top. Then, the books evicted the family. But now what a magnificent setting for a meeting of minds and broken hearts.

Baa
You were always the driver of the train. I was always in one of the carriages. Always. A daughter describing her father. The nervousness in the reading. The moist eyes. And the reassuring touch.

Taa
A bullet pierces flesh and an orange. Blood juice flows.

Thaa
Bodies stacked like photographs after they've been tossed in the air. The photos and the bodies. Memories fading like the real or imagined deformities of the dead. This is not a police procedural.

Djim
Who is the Dragoman? Is he like the bogey man? Or is he Adropos
who moves in mysterious ways.

Ghaa
The Imam's daughter. Another daughter. Chiding her principal to
heed her principals.

Ghor
Viewing the world through the slits of the lookout. I can see them
but they cannot see me. The difference between omnipotence and
impotence is a few letters.

Dhal
A woman confronting her own nudity. And the man within
enticing her. Why do I feel so guilty?

Thal
The hitchhiker. On a journey. And so are we.

Raa
On the shelves the beautiful photo of the bride surrounded by
books. Did the marriage survive? Maybe. Maybe not. But our love
affair with books. That is a different story.

Zaa
The mood music. The succulent food. The writers great and about
to be great. A divided capital. A unified gathering. If only things
could be so simple.

THE MISSING HOUR

Hakan Djuma

All souls in this city live in a loop. The loop has eleven hours. A perfect circle with eleven numbers. Quiet Mr Soldier Walls, beautiful Mrs Rooftile Cats, joyful Miss Sparrow Date, well respected Sir Man Minaret and Madame Loud Bells, all live in this city where clocks have eleven hours. I walked around to ask why.

'So that I can finish my military duty quicker and leave to see my loved ones who live outside the city' said Mr Soldier Walls when I sat with him for a cigarette.

'But your loved ones outside this city are aging quicker than you are as they have more hours in a day, this does not worry you?' I asked.

He said 'That's why I smoke so much. So that I can age at the same speed they do.'

He was indeed looking older than he actually was. His lips were dry as he licked the edge of cigarette paper. There were three lines between his eyebrows all going in different directions but without intersecting. I left my newly-bought tobacco with him and started walking towards the neighbourhoods where houses still have roofs.

She was sitting at the doorway of her house with an inviting dress and posture but with a sad look on her face. I said, 'You must be Mrs Rooftile Cats?'

'Yes, young man, how much would you give?' she asked with a fake smile on her face.

'I am here to hear your story of eleven hours,' I replied.

She apologised and said, 'I was not always like this, you know. When the men in your family die, the men of other families take advantage of you. After my father went missing my mother cried every night. It was also at night when they called to tell me that my husband had died. He stepped on a mine in the buffer zone. He was grazing animals, and instead of sending the animals to check he wanted to check himself if the fields were clean of the mines. You know, nights are shorter when you have eleven hours', she said. Her house was dark with no windows, and I could smell the humidity. The only way to have some sunlight inside this house would have been by removing the rooftop. There were three thriving pots of plants, which was surprising, considering the lack of sunlight. She saw me looking at the plants and she said, 'I feel sad sometimes that they are trapped in their pots. But it's only their roots that are trapped, and the leaves are free to grow, right?' I left her and walked towards the neighbourhood where birds chirp amongst the date trees.

Miss Sparrow Dates was very young. She was hanging laundry to dry on a rope that went from one date tree to two other date trees, creating a triangle. I asked, 'Why live in a city with eleven hours?'

She said, 'My parents came here with a special agreement, you know. We can save the hours and spend them when we go back to our own country.'

'But this is not fair', I said. 'You have to work eleven hours to earn one hour?' She replied with a smile on her face.

'We don't need much, we are happy with what we have.' I thought of the date trees. They need almost no water. They produce a lot of dirt and they have almost no shade, but they look beautiful on the landscape from some distance. Small birds come and hide inside them, sacrificing their freedom for security. Some birds are too small to fight for their own security, which is why they migrate in swarms. I started walking towards the city's richest neighbourhood.

Sir Man Minaret and Madame Loud Bells have been married since the beginning of time and have always lived in an enormous house, which can be seen from every part of the city. They are the richest people in the city and everybody respects them. They earned their wealth by selling painkillers. I found them sitting under a gigantic clock with eleven numbers when I entered their house. The hour hand of the clock was in the shape of a minaret , and the minute hand was in the shape of a church tower. I asked them 'Why eleven hours?' Sir Man Minaret replied,

'We have many patients, you know. You can't just give them painkillers and send them away, you also need to make them believe that the painkillers are effective. We do this by making music, otherwise the painkillers won't work.' Madame Loud Bells interrupted.

'He thinks singing makes them feel better. I think the sound of bells is more therapeutic. We needed to adjust our timing for the singing and the bell peels so they don't happen at the same time. I ring bells as long as the sun is visible in the sky and he sings for as long as the moon is visible in the sky. When there were twelve hours, there was one crossover hour when both the moon and the sun were in that sky together. So we removed that hour, and now we never make sounds together.'

I said, 'But you removed that hour also from the lives of the people who are curing these illnesses your painkillers treat.' They replied at the same time.

'More work for us, then.'

The next patient knocked the door three times, and my time was up.

I was thinking as I walked out of the city how brave fear is.

LEAVING NICOSIA, PART SIX
(FROM TIME ZONES)

Antoine Cassar

Insomma mister airport border guard
as this conversation continues in my head
waiting for you to return my passport
so I can fly to the city
in which I was born a foreigner
I'd like to tell you how uplifting it was
to ride along the streets of Nicosia
with friends from Cyclists Across Barriers
my beard rinsed in the breeze
that softens the walls of the labyrinth

In Bird Standard Time
it was the late afternoon thermals
I saw a wide-winged bird
glide with ease over the ruins
of the Armenian Quarter
and of no-man's land

In Cat Standard Time
it was the early evening stir
I saw a tricolour cat roaming
around and across the buffer zone
what we call in Maltese

a *qattusa tal-madonna*
a holy Mary cat
what in Cypriot Greek I believe you call
a *πατσάλα*
which crossed into the Cypriot Turkish
batsali
mottled, spotted, with smears of colour
white, orange, black
like the patches of a political map
of Cyprus for example
without counting the buffer zone
or if you prefer
without counting, for example
the British sovereign bases

To be honest, mister border guard
I should admit
I also thoroughly enjoyed
being able to show my passport
at both border booths
without coming off the bike seat
it's better than standing here waiting
you seem quite friendly
but please, hand me back the passport
so I can go rest my legs
at the departure gate
so they'll be ready to hit afresh
the ground they learnt to walk on

Efharistó
thanks and goodnight
with a slight cordial pinch

of the tip of my beret
now back on my head
warming my thoughts again

HIGH FIVE

Zoe Piponides

Hi, haven't seen you in ages!
How about a coffee?
Your place or mine?
Let's meet half way.
Checkpoint Café?
Fine. Time?
Around five?
Your five o'clock or my five o'clock?
Halve the difference?
Mine 4.30, yours 5.30?
Sounds good to me.

A WASTE OF TIME

Argyro Nicolaou

He could feel the sweat clinging to his armpits as he made his way to the checkpoint. He regretted wearing a shirt and blazer. The weather was much less chilly than his weather app had led him to believe, and he knew he would not escape the embarrassment of sweat patches under his arms and probably on his chest, too.

Ledra Street was unusually quiet. It was early on a Monday afternoon and most people hadn't left their jobs yet. The cafés he passed by were almost empty, with the exception of a group of teenagers huddled around a table at a Starbucks, smoking.

He was already late. They had set the meeting for 4pm. He left the office early, right after lunch, claiming he wasn't feeling well and needed to go to the doctor. He went home, took a long shower, and spent a good part of an hour trying to decide what to wear. The truth was that he had felt so nervous all morning he hadn't done much work anyway.

He never thought of himself as an adventurous person. He always assumed that his personal life would follow a predictable path, like his career. He studied Business Management in Leeds, then worked for four years at an audit firm in London, where he became a chartered accountant. He had returned to Cyprus three years ago, and had worked at his uncle's accounting firm ever since.

When he first met Neşe he didn't know her name. His cousin had dragged him to a beginners' tango class to support Natalie, their high school friend who had just returned from Buenos Aires with a tango teaching qualification. He tried telling her that he didn't look like a person who danced tango – he was on the short side, slightly balding, and the most fashionable item he owned was a brown leather sling-over briefcase his mother had bought for him in Milan two years ago – but she brushed him off. He went because he had nothing better to do, and didn't want to say no to his cousin. They worked together.

Neşe was at the tango class with two other women. She towered above them, her long black hair tied in a thick ponytail behind her back. Every time she said 'I'm sorry' to each of her dance partners she let out a soft chuckle that tickled his ears. When the dancers had rotated enough times for them to finally dance together, they were both too intent on looking at their feet to introduce themselves.

'Can you believe those three girls were Turkish Cypriot?' said his cousin early the following day.

He still hadn't taken the first sip of his morning coffee.

'Not that I care or anything. I just wish that I had known beforehand because I haven't met a Turkish Cypriot before.'

That first sip went a long way.

'Which girls?'

'The tall one, with the other two.'

He knew immediately who his cousin was talking about.

'Apparently her name's Neşe. Neşe! That's cool, right? She's friends with Natalie.'

Later that afternoon he went on the tango school's Facebook page and started searching for her. She was easy to find. Her profile picture showed a big, thick braid running down the middle of her back. He couldn't bear the thought of messaging her directly, so he scanned the page for a comment she might have made, or a picture she was tagged in.

He found one of her and Natalie from 2014 at the tango school's entrance. 'Can't get this one to start dancing!' said the caption. He couldn't comment on that; it would make him look like a creep. He liked the page and logged out of Facebook. He decided that learning tango wasn't such a bad idea.

When he went to class the following week, Neşe wasn't there. He left the studio as soon as the class was over, ignoring Natalie's invitation to go out for drinks with the rest of the group.

At home, he fell on the couch without having a shower, took his shoes off and started downloading the latest Liam Neeson movie. His phone pinged.

'Natalie says ur a really bad student for not coming out with us!'

He squinted to make out the thumbnail. It was Neşe. He sat up, his laptop falling to the floor. He typed and erased more than three different responses before settling on the least risky.

'Hey! wasn't feeling very well ... U having fun?'

'Yes, it's OK. See u next week then!'

Fuck. His jaw clenched and he started grinding his teeth. He should've said something witty about her being the bad student for not showing up. Or something self-deprecating. He went to the kitchen, opened the fridge and grabbed three slices of cheddar cheese, putting all of them in his mouth at once. When he was done he went back to the couch and picked up his phone, mortified.

'See ya.'

The Liam Neeson movie was pretty shit. As the credits were rolling, his phone pinged again.

'Unless u want to have a coffee tmrw? It's my day off.'

They set a meeting point under the clocks in the north part of Nicosia, close to the Ledra checkpoint. He had never been there before, but didn't tell her. He planned on getting to the checkpoint fifteen minutes earlier, just in case he got lost and needed the extra time to find the place.

Instead he was late. He had spent too long in the shower, too long picking his outfit, which she wouldn't be able to tell anyway because he had sweated so much he looked like he'd come straight from work.

At the checkpoint he waited for ten minutes in the wrong queue. A group of German tourists were crossing from the north to the south, and their excitement was causing a delay. When he finally got to the window of the police cubicle, the Greek Cypriot policeman laughed at him and pointed to another set of cubicles further along in the buffer zone.

'You haven't been here before? Go over there. And relax.'

He gave his ID to a Turkish Cypriot policewoman and looked at his watch. 4.15pm. She stamped some papers and returned the ID. It was that simple. He followed Neşe's instructions and walked in a straight line. They gave him a sense of purpose, hiding the fact that he had no idea where he was, even if this side of the checkpoint didn't seem all that different to the side he had just come from.

Only a few metres away from him was a small square, with a circle of benches around a post with many signs on it. They all pointed in different directions, leading to places he didn't know. The only place name he recognized was that of Büyük Han.

Above the benches he saw the outlines of three big clocks. He assumed this was the right place and immediately started looking around for Neşe. She wasn't sitting on any of the benches. She wasn't looking at things to buy at the nearby merchant stalls. She wasn't standing in line for a coffee at any of the many coffee shops in the square.

She had probably left. Fifteen minutes is a long time to wait for someone you hardly know. He sat on the bench closest to him, facing a narrow street lined with tables of colourful souvenirs. He brought his palms to the sides of his face, trying to relax his jaw by massaging the joints under his ears with his fingers. He looked at his watch. 4.23pm. He opened the Messenger app on his phone, and started typing: 'Hey, I was late ... Sorry I missed u. I'm here now if ur around.' He decided not to send it.

He would wait until 5pm. He bent his head forward and then back, trying to ease the tension in his neck. Two bean-shaped sweat patches had formed on his chest, one on each side.

At 4.55pm he stood up to leave. He looked around one last time. He dragged his feet to the checkpoint on the opposite side of the street and gave his ID. He hadn't noticed that the clock in the square read 5.55pm.

WHY ARE GREEN LINES
CALLED GREEN?

Jacqueline Jondot

Why are green lines called green
When they are drawn with the charred remains of homes?

Why are green lines called green
When they are dusty with the dried-up flow of sap?

Why are green lines called green
When they are scarred with the metallic grey of barbed wire?

Why are green lines called green
When they are whitish blue from the droppings of wary doves?

Why are green lines called green
When they are stark blue and white lines of emptied barrels?

They are called green lines
When palm trees join palms across the void

They are called green lines
When love songs replace howling bullets

They are called green lines
When laden trees fill the dun dead dusty gap with luscious figs

They are called green lines
When voice answers voice in no man's land

They are called green lines
When pomegranate clusters turn into the red fruit of rebirth

BEYOND BARRIERS

Maria Kitromilidou

A soul's journey into the unknown
Deep within unfolding
The colours of walking
The familiar
The joint journeys
The love shared
All that unites
Deep within unfolding
A sweet confusion
Wishful thoughts
New memories

NICOSIA THROUGH THE EYES OF A CHILD

Sherry Charlton

We arrived at night. I can feel it in my body, even now.

Stepping out of the propeller plane, down the metal steps onto the tarmac of Nicosia International Airport, I was enveloped by the unexpected warmth of a night air rich with jasmine, pine and eucalyptus: fragrances I know now, but did not know then. And the bright lights, a sky full of stars, insects – cicadas – singing loudly. Airport workers watched our arrival. A strikingly handsome man came to greet us, immaculate in airline uniform. A black cap, white shirt, brown shining skin. Dark eyes, thick black curls. That was Nick Kalimantianos. As a child, I was entranced by this vision of male beauty. Inside his car, his confident voice welcomed us to Nicosia. I was five and a half and I was in heaven. We were transported away from the airport lights, towards the unknown depths of this new city, our new home far from our prefab in Gatwick Green, Bishop's Stortford. It was 1955, Dad was an aircraft engineer and had a new job with Cyprus Airways.

Desperately lonely, missing the closeness of her Gatwick Green friends, Mum became ill after a few weeks with a vicious dose of pneumonia from which, she told me years later, she nearly died. She remembers being drawn towards a red light, feeling afraid. A moment came when she stopped moving towards it. That was when her fever broke, and she survived. She was thirty-two. She is now ninety-five.

Our first home in Nicosia was 5 Scra Street. It had cool stone floors and a musty smell. Transparent lizards – geckos – slithered up the walls. The rooms were always dark during the day, closed in behind green wooden shutters. It seemed strange to us, but they shut out the sun and lessened the stifling heat. Our neighbourhood in Nicosia was mixed – there were British, American, Greek and Turkish Cypriot families. As new arrivals we felt certain attitudes from some people. An American family lived next door. Robyn, their only child, was a pretty, fairy-like blonde girl. She was younger than me but seemed to know everything. Her parents made a great fuss of her and didn't really like me at all. I was ginger-haired, freckly and a 'tomboy'. Her father had an important job in Nicosia, so they told us. We weren't the 'right kind' of people.

The Masons lived further down the road. Chaotic, warm and friendly, grubby, tousled-haired children, they were always happy and welcoming. One particularly hot day, I ran from our house to visit them. I had gone a short distance before I felt the melted tarmac on the pavement burning into my bare feet. Getting home was terrifying and painful. I got blisters. Mum was criticised by some people for not putting me in shoes. There was a set of people who kept themselves apart and looked down on everyone. Some worked at the 'Secretariat' and had big cars. They didn't let their children go barefoot. That would make them look like 'the locals'. I wasn't sure who they were or where they lived but I felt their judgement. I imagined they lived in large houses, up on a hill somewhere.

Once, I was invited to play with a neighbour's child; a titian-haired Greek girl called Michela. I didn't know her well. I remember their back yard with her elderly relatives dressed in black. I felt awkward and self-conscious as I didn't speak Greek. A cat had just given birth and the tomcat was attacking the kittens. Everyone was screaming frantically but doing nothing to help the poor little things. Feeling helpless and scared, I stepped back and the grisly scene disappeared as, still vertical, I plummeted down a ten-foot drop to the concrete floor of the cellar entrance. I could have died, my Mum said. I fretted forever about the kittens and I couldn't bring myself to visit Michela again.

Behind our house there were fields with scrubby grass and grazing sheep. I loved wandering over there on my own. I liked the sound of bells as the sheep moved lazily between clumps of straw-like grass and the feel of warm air on my arms and legs. There were houses dotted around, all different and not in rows. The Crown Hotel lingered all on its own, with grey and dark red walls. The scene repeated and quietly went on forever, no walls or fences, nothing blocking or carving the landscape. This place had its own peace and the sheep fitted in well. I could breathe in this space.

The Mermaid restaurant was nearby. It was lit by a beautiful figure of a mermaid who cast a mesmerising shimmer of blue light above the entrance. Seeing it at night always gave me a thrill. Mum and Dad were invited to dinner there one evening. It was so exciting watching them both get dressed up, Dad so handsome in a navy suit and his hair Brylcreemed back, and Mum beautiful in her floral dress. I saw their excitement as we waved 'goodbye'. They came back early, and the next day I overheard them sharing the story with another couple. The restaurant had been evacuated after a bomb scare. The bomb was found strapped under a table, near Mum and Dad's.

I heard the word 'curfew' a lot. I had no idea what it was. Whenever we were notified of one, everything outside stopped and went strangely quiet. Parts of the town and surrounding areas were regularly closed off. Dad tried explaining it without scaring me, but I picked up on the danger. I just didn't know what we were supposed to be scared of, and that made it feel more unsafe.

One morning we woke to find armed soldiers in the ditch

outside our house. Mum and Dad had heard there had been an 'incident'. I couldn't go to school. We all had to stay indoors. I wasn't scared, just curious. I wondered what the 'incident' was. There were often British soldiers around, with guns and stern faces. They were packed into the back of large covered trucks as we drove behind them. We sometimes saw them drinking and being rowdy. Mum tells me now she was always nervous around the soldiers, sensing their volatility. She would stay quiet and calm around them to ensure Mandy and I felt safe.

Nicosia, the old town, fascinated me. Voices chattering in different tongues, strains of unfamiliar music; car horns blasting, passing through crowded streets. All sorts of faces, some scorched and lined, some fresh and brown, laughing and shouting. I felt like a pioneer, alone but brave, exploring those narrow side streets packed with tiny shops overflowing with anything and everything. I felt sorry for the skinny dogs diving into doorways to avoid donkeys and carts.

The onslaught of colours and shapes in the market was a new visual language. The scents of unfamiliar fruits and vegetables were overwhelming. Some made me feel sick, but later, I was drawn to them and the memories they held. Metaxas Square: even its name sounded ancient and comforting. The roads there were wide, the shops large and shiny. I used to have my hair cut by a lady named Anna in a salon. On one occasion she seemed agitated and hacked wildly at my hair. When Mum intervened, she threw down the scissors crossly and disappeared. I looked like a little urchin boy. I was so upset and embarrassed to be seen like that.

Greek Orthodox priests both intrigued and terrified me. They were dressed from head to foot in black. I thought they held some invisible power, those tall, mute figures, striding through the streets. People lowered their heads to them, some kissed their hands. I knew they were linked in some way to God, but I was scared by what was hidden within the black robes. Later I became aware of Archbishop Makarios. He was constantly on the radio. My parents discussed him in connection with 'the troubles'. As a child, I only knew that 'the troubles' were grown-up people on different sides trying to win and hurting each other.

I have an eerie memory of a young Cypriot man being hung in the prison. He was called Bobby something. We heard prisoners chanting their protest all afternoon. It was awful. Suddenly there was silence, the chanting stopped. We knew that was the moment he died. I remember feeling sick, knowing what had happened. Mum cried. She was angry too. She carries those sounds and that moment of silence with her to this day, and she visibly shudders when asked to recall it.

My school, 'Sessions', was surrounded by bamboo plants. It was owned by the headmistress Miss Sessions. She was neat, precise and English. My teacher Miss Kavorkian was Armenian. Everything about her was dark brown – her hair, her eyes, even her lips were reddish brown – but her skin was a translucent white. She often looked nervous and far away. I was shy of her at first, but she was kind and I grew to like her. Suphi Sies was assigned to look after me when I arrived as 'the new girl'. He was Turkish Cypriot. He had gentle eyes and held my hand protectively at playtimes. I trusted him, unlike Angus, the loud boy with blond hair and a large floppy mouth who got badly chastised for standing on a chair in the classroom and shouting 'EOKA!' out of the window. I wondered what *eoka* meant.

Tefik Fikret Street became our permanent home in Nicosia. We rented from Kamran, who lived next door with her elderly parents, Mama and Papa Aziz, as we called them. Kamran was a pharmacist with her own shop in town. Years later, I learnt that she was also a composer and a well-known *kanun* player, who gave concerts. She always looked very elegant and smoked a cigarette through a long black holder. She visited Mum and Dad some evenings. They would sit on the veranda and share Keo beers. Kamran often looked serious, but Dad's humour tickled her. She would fling her head back and laugh, so happy and so beautiful.

Mama and Papa Aziz loved Mandy and me. They would coo at us and fondle our hair. Papa Aziz smiled and made kind clucking sounds. I understand now that adults in Cyprus did this to babies and children. I remember his gentleness. He was the scientist who eradicated malaria in Cyprus, working for the Colonial Service. Grown-ups were noticeably affectionate and loving towards us. They didn't seem to find us annoying or tell us to 'run and play'. Nene helped Mum in our home a few times a week. She was a large and comforting woman, quite shy. Dad would attempt to speak Turkish to her. She would giggle. I learnt that Nicosia had a Turkish and a Greek 'sector'. Like us, Nene lived in the Turkish sector, but when 'the troubles' were bad, Dad would drive her home to make sure she was safe.

Our home in Nicosia meant freedom and adventure when not at school. Beyond Kamran's house, a track led to a part of the town's moat. It was supposedly out of bounds, but I would secretly meet up there with friends to have 'adventures'. The metal girder which straddled the gulley was the width of a shoe. We dared each other to walk across. It could have gone terribly wrong but we all managed to cross unharmed. The moat in the town had a play-park. I didn't like the big swings but the double rocking chairs, with little benches at either end, were quite hypnotic. The shiny brown rockinghorse with seats along its back was a favourite. Dad would lift Mandy up, but she was unsure. She was only fourteen months old. Some kids would race from ride to ride, like me. I noticed others, dressed more formally, sitting with parents, just watching. I felt sorry for them. The moat circled the city of Nicosia. Maybe other children were playing similar games further round?

Years after my time there, I discovered that while I was exploring my world in Tefik Fikret Street, a short step away in Hilal Street, another little girl, three years older, was also living and playing in Nicosia. She also played on the brown horse in the moat playground. The inter-weaving lives that passed through Nicosia still amaze me. We didn't know each other then, but in 1968 we met on a bus going into Cardiff. We were both starting at the University. I was politically naive and unsophisticated, on my way to the Fresher's Ball. She was politically astute and fiercely knowledgeable, on her way to distribute leaflets to the miners in the valleys. As different as we were, we shared a deep affection for Cyprus and for Nicosia. Our friendship began right there. Three years later, after finals, three of us hitch-hiked from Cardiff to Nicosia, an epic journey, another story. Aydın and I remain deep friends to this day. My life would be so much poorer without her in it.

My cousin Gillian came to live with us in Nicosia in 1957. She met Elie, a cherished family friend who was a Palestinian Christian, born in Haifa. His entire family were displaced from their homes after Britain was instrumental in creating the state of Israel, forcing the Palestinian people to become refugees; a brutal, reckless move. Elie's family fled to Cyprus. They were professional people who spoke many languages, dignified and proud. Elie was such a gentle and loving man. Recalling his sweetness towards us as children still melts my heart. He was a talented cook who taught me how to handle food with respect. I learned from him how to make the best *tabouleh*. Gillian introduced Elie to her family in Maldon, where they were married. They had two children, each of whom has two children. I remain in touch with some of Elie's Palestinian relatives.

We also became close to the family of Jimmy McLean, who worked alongside Dad at Nicosia Airport. We enjoyed picnics, parties, and travelling the island together. Mum still talks about the beautiful times they shared when they were all so young. We returned to England in 1958. A year later, Jimmy arrived from Cyprus with his family, to work alongside Dad at Gatwick Airport. Jimmy visited us regularly over the years. When Dad died in 1973, Mum was devastated and Jimmy's world crashed. They remained friends and supported each other. Years later, Mum and Jimmy married. They spent twelve happy years together before Jimmy passed away. Nicosia gave us this; it gave people permission to enjoy life and the courage to engage. An intangible bond is shared by those of us who were connected in that time and place.

PETRICHOR REQUIEM

Salamis Aysegul Sentug

'en garde' said the barefoot man, 'and count till three'
worms on his head threatening, not me
no one could threaten someone
who is celebrating
the last day in a society, of any kind
vulturous, unless you are
a lucky homeless
lucky that he could live
with everything he resists.

'they caught me
the moments
at the moment they caught me
they were shadowless
slyly penetrating in memories
carried by dystopian stories
ever written or deadly lived.
they caught me
I am the last one survived
and they told me
even D 503 managed to die
everything has abandoned its ultimate aim
here, on the Lefkonos Street
the cloud valley of smoked dreams
is hanging from the wings

of a singing grass finch
peace. peace. peace.
reminding the beauty of measuring time
via space that no longer exists
it is raining
I am wet
they are all working
for a better death
– which is a forgotten crime –
or to disregard time
that no longer means a thing
for a being who is unearthing
secret facts on being a warder in her own mind.
I was really close to the border,
I was really close
they caught me.
my sense of time through the lit puddle
is gradually diminishing now
no one is walking in the rain
and life's sense out of me
is diminishing from time
I was really close
I was really close, they caught me
"all the others are dead"
"all the protagonists"
said the ponderous one
proudly wearing a hat bigger than his head
one more day, they gave me
to say farewell
to Frangias, to Orwell.'

on the way to the border

I found an acorn of an invisible tree
opened in my hands, beautifully
the very last afternoon,
at the ivory tower of daytime
I sat down next to the homeless man
'how rich this acorn smells
these ones have olfactory power,
these ones, from trees close to the border'
I closed my eyes, whiff,
and counted until three.
'which acorn' he asked 'of which trees?'
'which border' I replied in silence.

LEDRA STREET CROSSING

Rachael Pettus

Neither side wants passports from the cats.
A sleek and careless tabby
has crossed and re-crossed twice
since I took my coffee
to a streetside table
near the checkpoint.

People
fill out papers, hand over documents,
and file through the checkpoints;
orderly, polite.
But ginger and calico,
white and pied,
cats pass unhindered.
They stroll past the queues
and jump the barricades,
or sit –
hind leg extended forward, toes stretched and claws displayed –
washing themselves
in the Dead Zone.

And the birds?
They flap from rooftops and balconies,
sing in the trees,
and weave between flagpoles

BLUE ANTS, RED ANTS

Elisa Bosio

The black Mercedes sedan ahead of us came to a slow halt by the side of the road. A few moments later, the vehicle my mother and I were in pulled up behind it and the driver turned the key in the ignition. Through the windshield, I watched my brother, Orestis, step out from the passenger side of the Mercedes while his wife and my eldest niece got out from the back seats. My gaze followed the driver of the car that had been awaiting the arrival of our convoy. The driver took a few steps towards Orestis; he had a long stride on account of his height. His face broke out into a warm smile as he shook my brother's hand, placing his other hand on Orestis's shoulder. Once again, I was struck with a feeling of déjà vu; I had experienced the sensation several times over the course of the past few hours. I shook my head, trying somehow to shake off the feeling. After all, I had seen that smile before, back in 1973. It was 2003 and I hadn't seen Cemil for thirty years.

Orestis and I had both attended a private, English-speaking high school in Nicosia and about 10 per cent of our classmates were Turkish-Cypriot. While I hadn't befriended any, Orestis had become good friends with Cemil, who he took chemistry with. Cemil was a tall, mild-mannered boy with kind, dark brown eyes. From time to time he would visit our house after school, politely accepting my mother's fresh pies and glasses of lemonade and chatting with me about my school work.

Cemil lived with his family in the Turkish-Cypriot enclave in Nicosia, and I would sometimes hear him talking about the hardships that they had to endure on account of various restrictions that had been placed upon them. Sometimes, he and Orestis would spend time sitting outside in our garden talking about politics and religion. They didn't mind if I joined them but I could tell that my father wasn't very keen on me spending time with them.

'Ate, come on, Eleni.' My mother's voice broke through my thoughts. Her hand lingered on the door handle as she looked at me. It had been a long, emotional morning for us all. When the crossing point had suddenly opened ten days ago, thousands of Cypriots were eager to visit the other side. Many were curious to see what had happened to their homes and villages after nearly three decades. My family was among the lucky ones. Ayios Pavlos, our neighbourhood, lay just south of the Green Line. Many relatives and family friends were not as fortunate. A couple of days after the checkpoint opened, my brother received a telephone call from Cemil, who suggested that they meet. They hadn't seen one another since high school. Our mother had expressed an interest in visiting the Apostolos Andreas Monastery in Rizokarpaso and, when Orestis mentioned this, Cemil had immediately suggested that we meet the following Saturday.

Orestis had picked us up earlier that morning and driven to Ledra Palace, parking a short distance from the imposing building that now served as barracks for the United Nations. Prior to the invasion, the five-storey structure was a glamorous hotel that hosted affluent individuals from across the region. As we walked past it towards the crossing point, I couldn't help but imagine the elegantly dressed men and women playing bridge or dancing in the ballroom during the 1950s and 60s. Today, barrels and barbed wire surround the building and a smattering of bullet holes marks the violence that had taken place there. My mother, brother, sister-in-law, niece and I walked in silence up the road. There were several people walking in the same direction, on a similar pilgrimage.

The early May morning was bright and unseasonably warm. The male cicadas' mating call echoed in the surrounding trees; an incessant, high-pitched song that accompanied us along the way. In my mind's eye, I pictured the city from above and drew an imaginary line around the Venetian walls that encircled the city, making sure to include the eleven bastions that stood out like flower bulbs. I chose a maroon crayon to mark the Green Line that cut my capital in half; a bleeding laceration that had not yet healed.

Once we had handed over our ID cards for inspection and completed the compulsory white paper slip that served as a 'visa', we found ourselves on the other side of the divide. Cemil was waiting for us with his family. Before any introductions could be made, Cemil enveloped Orestis in a long embrace, withdrawing only to keep both hands on my brother's arms. His eyes searched his face for a long moment before they crinkled up as a smile spread from cheek to cheek.

'It's good to see you, friend.'

Orestis turned to introduce his wife and daughter and to re-introduce my mother and me. I took a moment to look around while the others discussed the itinerary. It felt incredibly surreal to be standing on the same street and yet for everything to seem so different. The pavement was painted differently, the stop sign at the end of the street was a different size and the signs above the store fronts were in a different language. I gazed up at the blue sky and back down at the orange trees that lined the street. They were familiar, similar, and this realisation settled me.

Over the course of the next few hours, we visited Apostolos Andreas, marvelling at the beauty of the untouched shoreline en route to the monastery. We then continued towards Famagusta, stopping for lunch nearby, before returning to Nicosia. My mother and I rode with Cemil's cousin and his wife, both of whom maintained a friendly banter with us in their uniquely accented English. Orestis and Cemil engaged in long conversations in an attempt to catch up on nearly three decades of experiences and stories. They reminisced about their days as students and spoke about the political situation and the possibility of a solution to the Cyprus Problem.

As we neared Nicosia, I reached for my mother's hand and gave it a squeeze. She had been quieter than usual. This was, in part, due to her being unable to contribute very much to the English conversation. I also attributed this to her wanting to take in as much as possible as she spent most of the time staring out the car window. I had fallen into the same pattern; I had not wanted to miss a moment. She glanced at me and smiled sadly. I could tell that the day had dredged up a lot of emotions and she looked quite frail beside me.

In a matter of minutes, we found ourselves back at the crossing point, thanking Cemil and his family for their hospitality. When it was her turn, my mother leaned forward and kissed Cemil. As we turned to walk back to our car, she looked at Orestis and let out a sigh. My brother raised an eyebrow, seeking an explanation from her, which she readily offered.

'Ach, Orestis ... Are you happy now? Did you enjoy having me kiss that filthy dog?'

***

I turned the pages of a local newspaper as I waited for my morning tea to steep. I could tell by the steam rising past the rim of the chipped mug that if I took a sip I would scald my tongue. It was a quiet, overcast Saturday morning in November 1983 and the only sound I could hear was the ticking of the grandfather clock in my living room. I glanced out the window at the green tree tops that stood just outside my third-floor apartment. It overlooked the Pedieos, the longest river in Cyprus, which flows through the capital. I remember reading that the river used to flow through the centre of the old town but had been diverted northwards by the Venetians during the 16th century.

I usually spend my Saturday mornings walking along the river bed, beneath the eucalyptus and palm trees that provide a green oasis in the middle of the city. This morning was no different. After returning from my walk, I settled down to read the newspaper. The front page was dominated by the government's reaction to the unilateral declaration of independence of the 'Turkish Republic of Northern Cyprus' five days earlier. The Security Council of the UN had met only two days later, describing the act as 'legally invalid' and calling for the withdrawal of the Declaration of Independence.

Several minutes passed and I realised that my tea had gone cold. Pushing back my chair, I stood and picked up the mug, making my way to the kitchen. I would have to make a fresh cup. As I waited for the kettle to boil, I recalled those terrible weeks nine summers ago when the Turkish troops had invaded. I had been seventeen years old at the time. Orestis, a couple of years older, had just finished high school and was undergoing his military service. My mother and father were beside themselves with worry knowing that he could find himself on the frontline of the fighting, which is exactly what had happened.

It took a couple of years for my brother to tell me what had happened during that summer in 1974, although we were close. On the morning of the invasion, he had received orders to make his way to Kyrenia during the early hours of Saturday, 20 July. They had received word of a Turkish attack, and soldiers from Nicosia were travelling north to be in position. My heart beat faster in my chest and my breath caught in my throat as he described being in a truck with several other soldiers who joked about the prospect of getting the chance to rape Turkish-Cypriot girls. When they arrived at their destination, they were ordered to shoot in the direction of the enemy. 'It was dark and the target was far away. There was no way of knowing what or who we were shooting at,' he said, speaking softly. Orestis and I never discussed his experience of the war after that.

***

I woke to the lingering smell of orange zest, cinnamon and nutmeg spice and roasted hazelnuts, having spent the previous afternoon and evening in our kitchen with my mother and Yiayia Eleni, my maternal grandmother, baking melomakarona, traditional Christmas honey cookies. It was 1963, and this year I was allowed to carefully stir all the ingredients that my mother had combined into a big bowl and to shape the dough into small circles, carefully pressing my thumb into the centre to form the dent in the middle of each cookie, which would later be topped with crushed nuts. Yiayia Eleni had been taught the recipe by her mother and it was passed down from one generation to another. She oversaw the entire process, from beginning to end, cautioning us whenever we failed to follow the steps exactly as she would. While I welcomed my grandmother's critique, my mother's clenched jaw told me that she was less open to her advice.

The next morning, I rolled over in my small single bed to see whether my brother, Orestis, was still asleep. His bed was empty and the sheets, as usual, were thrown back and rumpled. The sunlight streaming through the slits in the dark-green wooden shutters indicated that it was past 8am. It was Saturday, and the first official day of the Christmas holidays. I couldn't wait to spend the day playing in the garden and, later, to play with my doll in the living room as our mother prepared dinner. My stomach growled, reminding me that it was time for breakfast. After making the beds, I made my way down the cool, dimly lit corridor that led to the kitchen and living room. I expected to find my mother in the kitchen, setting breakfast out for us. However, it was empty and the square wooden table in the middle of the room was bare.

I continued into the living room and found my parents and grandmother sitting together on the sofa, whispering quietly amongst themselves. Orestis was sitting at the dining room table reading his history textbook. He looked up at me as I entered the room. I rolled my eyes at him. At nine years old, he was two years older than me and always had his nose in a book. I looked over at the adults and then back at him, raising a questioning eyebrow. He gave a slight shrug of his shoulder and went back to reading.

Was someone ill? At that moment, my mother noticed me in the room. Noting the expression on my face, she rose quickly and came towards me, placing her hands on my shoulders and leading me back towards the kitchen.

'*Kalimera, agapi mou*, are you hungry? Let me make you some breakfast.' Looking over her shoulder, she called, '*Oresti mou*, come along. You need to eat too.'

A few minutes later, Orestis and I were devouring the fried eggs, sliced cucumbers and tomatoes that our mother had prepared for us. When she left to tend to the laundry, I leaned forward and whispered, 'What happened, Oresti? Why are they so serious?'

He told me that our uncle Marios had come by earlier in the morning. Orestis had overheard our uncle and father on the balcony as they smoked their cigarettes. Uncle Marios was describing how some people had been attacked in the middle of the night in the centre of the city.

Mother spent the rest of the morning and early afternoon tidying up the house and changing our bed sheets, which I found odd as she typically did so on Mondays. She explained that some relatives were coming to stay with us and that they would be sleeping in our room. We would have to sleep on makeshift beds on our parents' bedroom floor. Orestis and I were annoyed at having to vacate our room, but the look on mother's face warned us not to complain about this. At least they could try my melomakarona cookies – I was secretly looking forward to receiving their compliments on how good they tasted.

The relatives arrived shortly before dinner, and uncle Marios and his family joined us as well. After dinner, the adults sat around the coffee table discussing the events of the day, while Orestis and I were sent to bed. After a few minutes of lying in the dark, neither one of us had fallen asleep. Quietly, we made our way down the corridor towards the living room. Careful to stay out of sight, we overheard the adults still deep in conversation. Uncle Marios's loud voice could be heard above the rest. 'The lads went into their villages and butchered them. They returned with bags full of chopped ears and noses! It was a sight to be seen! That will teach those Turks not to mess with us.'

Upon hearing this, I let out a small gasp. Afraid that someone might have heard us, Orestis and I hurried back to our parents' bedroom, lay down and pretended to be asleep. I could feel my heartbeat ringing in my ears. A few moments passed, but no one came. As my eyes adjusted to the darkness, I turned to see Orestis looking at me.

'Will the Turks come and cut us up now?' I whispered.

'No, they won't. They live far from here and uncle Marios and father won't let anyone hurt us,' he replied confidently, taking my hand in his own. I nodded silently and closed my eyes willing myself to sleep.

That night, I dreamt that we were playing in the field near

our house. We were looking for ants to trample on in the dirt, a pastime that would happily engage us for hours. There were two types of ants: blue-black ants and red-black ants. The red-black ones had a habit of rising up on their hind legs as if ready to strike us back. We were careful to spare the blue-black ants; we only killed the red-black variety.

FIRST CALL

Marianna Foka

Heart of the city you have heard the whispers of generations
In the daytime all is noise against the glaring Mediterranean heat
In the night one by one sounds are traced in the breeze
Tyres screech and sirens wail
Dogs baying and cats mewling
All funnelling towards the break of day
There is but a beckoning
Synchronous and sonorous
The muezzin's tall tower
The church's arching dome
The waking alarms to God
Heart of the city you have heard the whispers of generations

BROKEN HEART

Stephanos Stephanides

on a twilight pilgrimage
I cross Venetian ramparts
I journey inward
seeking a language of lament
a muffled murmuring of old heart
graffiti on old walls
our dreams are in the tombs
tombs are in our dreams

eyes blind and eager
jalousies hiding light of white courtyards
ghosts of mustachioed men striding wicker chairs
muddied destinies at the bottom of coffee cups
shadows of grandmothers in the memory of lemon-trees
arthritic hands still joining my quilt piece piece

shielding my body
stone uterus of weeping icons
Byzantine saints whose names I don't recall
only a memory a fragrance of ancient smoking leaves
and wailing prayers of unseen *hodjas* to the north

warm countenance of youth in cold helmets
is the lifeline of this ailing heart
fluttering banners

that banish me from severed arteries
and I move outward through the city gates
while I dream of east and north
of apparitions of community
a communion
with sea citrus milk of sheep
and olive
in a dawning waning earth
fragile trophy of my quest

THE STORY OF THE DEAD ZONE

Yiannis Papadakis

A line ran through walled Nicosia in medieval maps; another through contemporary ones. The two lines were almost identical, dividing the city along an east–west axis. The line crossing the medieval city was a river. Later through human effort it became a long bridge; later still, through more human toil, it was to turn into a chasm, a dangerous no man's land. It still remains a site of division and contact: the paradox of borders.

The river was called by various names: proper and improper, official ones appearing on maps and unofficial ones that people used, clean and dirty, Turkish Cypriot and Greek Cypriot. The proper name Greek Cypriots used was Pedieos (from *pediada*, meaning plain) but they were colloquially called Pithkias. Most Greek Cypriots knew it that way, and some Turkish Cypriots too. Among Turkish Cypriots it was also called Kanli Dere, meaning 'Bloody Torrent'. They also called it Chirkefli Dere ('Foul Torrent'), while Greek Cypriots used an even stronger name, Kotsirkas ('Turd-carrier'). It has lived up to all its names.

The river flowed through the city walls until 1567, when the Venetians diverted its course for strategic reasons. During the Ottoman period, the old riverbed running through the walled city was left open. The Ottoman administrative centre lay north of the empty riverbed, with the Orthodox one on the south. Powerful Muslim and Christian families congregated around the two administrative centres on either side of the riverbed. It was during these times that the river acquired the Turkish name Kanli

Dere ('Bloody Torrent'), on account of the red hue of its water, on the occasions when it still flowed. Later, it took on the other two dirtier names, one in Turkish and the other in Greek, due to the refuse it carried along. By that time, it only followed the course through Nicosia occasionally, when rains were heavy. When the British took over in 1878, the old riverbed was gradually covered up for hygiene reasons and a road was paved above it, effectively serving the purpose of a long bridge over the riverbed.

This road was called Hermes Street. It became the major commercial axis of the city, bringing people of different groups together for trade. Hermes was the ancient Greek god of traders, and appropriately, he is also associated with Hades and the Kingdom of the Dead, the ancient Greeks' own Zone of the Dead. One of Hermes' epithets is Psychopompos ('the bearer of souls to Hades'), for he could cross the most difficult boundaries, including the one between the living and the dead. After 1963, the Green Line emerged along Hermes Street as the Dead Zone was born, first drawn by a British officer in green. Hermes Street became a savagely fought-over boundary, its ground drenched in blood.

It was not long before the Dead Zone that Hermes Street acquired its own Cerberus. Cerberus Street lay at the edge of the Tahtakallas district. Before the area's Turkish Cypriot inhabitants abandoned Tahtakale in 1964, the street had a Turkish name, Chinar Sokak, or 'Plane Tree Street'. It was changed by Greek Cypriots.

A few years after 1974, this river-bridge returned to its old ways. The old underground riverbed became the main artery of the jointly administered sewerage system. It became the city's main carrier of dirt and a site of underground cooperation. On the ground a site of bloodshed and danger: underground a project of mutual benefit where the two sides came together in their joint handling of excrement.

Later, the Dead Zone became a site of underground cooperation above ground also. The Leda Palace Hotel, which lay just outside the old city walls, next to the riverbed, was the only point of contact and communication between the two sides. During the early 1990s, the Ledra Palace, which was managed by the UN, was the only safe site where people from the two sides of Cyprus could meet. The meetings took place quietly within the Dead Zone because those of us who participated were branded as traitors on both sides: the predicament of those located within boundaries.

A WALK THROUGH LEDRA

Kivanc Houssein

'Nicosia? Why would you want to go to Nicosia? It's a city –
too hot, too dry, why the other side? ... stay here. Eat! Go to the
beach!' All that rang in my ears, and, as my suitcase dragged over
the uneven cobblestones in the early morning heat, I was starting
to think they were right. But I wanted to see and feel and hear
Nicosia for myself, to put my open-mindedness to the test. Who
would prevail: the village bigot or the village idiot? And whilst I
don't mind being called the village idiot, being the village bigot
full of hate and bile wouldn't sit right with me.

'*Parakalo*' the checkpoint guard said to me. I thought he
meant 'just walk right through'. No. A second, sterner '*parakalo*'
aided this time by forceful hand gestures clearly indicated 'I want
to look through your case'. Nothing my polite smile and lack of
contraband tobacco couldn't fix. His hand did hover agonisingly
over my bottle of absinthe ... but his hand moved away, and after
a sweaty repacking of my bag, I walked up Ledras Street and into
my first shock. An actual McDonalds and right next to it a Starbucks. Not a 'Mickdonots' or 'Starbuds' as I had become accustomed to on the North side. Even more surreal, a group of Phil-
ippine women on their day off from work were out taking selfies.
This, along with the heat, confused me. Is this Cyprus? It could be
Costa Del British Highroad. I didn't succumb to the franchises,
instead opting for a wholesome Cypriot breakfast at the hotel. Far
more satisfying and a whole lot less McCholesterol.

Refreshed and re-clothed, I met my guide who was eloquent,

knowledgeable and wise. Our first port of call was all air-conditioning and cocktails infused with spices and herbs for a catch-up chat. Just by being there, I felt chic. Then it was back to the bustling Ledras Street, and it struck me again how modern and up to date this main artery of Nicosia was. We ended up near the border crossing at a quaint little café for fresh homemade lemonade and just-out-the-oven cheese pies. Normality to the right, sandbags to the left. Sandbags and barbed wire and the green line; a reminder of what it means to be Nicosia: the only divided capital city in the world.

A peephole has been left in the sandbags. A bit of history, there in front of your eyes should you want to look: 1974, dishevelled, desolate, abandoned. Broken down by forty-two years of sun, covered in forty-two years of hot dust. Silent. Our leaders should negotiate there in the very palpable results of this division, not in chandelier-lit plush committee rooms wearing suits and ties. They should sit on rickety village chairs with tepid water and hash out a deal or let the dust settle on them too. I wonder if the green line runs the same course as today's mostly dry Pedieos River, which, unlike this green line, used to run life-giving through the city.

It takes a while for time travel to work its way out of your system. Meeting up with friends for my first taste of *souvlaki* pulls me back to the here and now. The meze, of course, I know and love, but the *souvlaki* … Chomp, yum lemon, squeeze, squirt in the eye, ahh stings, tears, succulent smell, yum, no talk, eat squeeze consume. Cypriots are not uncomfortable with just eating. Sated we talk, this mixed table of Greeks and Turks, and our conversation reveals a multitude of shared words, parental attitudes, social attitudes, love of food, love of country. The voices surrounding us are multi-lingual: Greek, Turkish, English, German and more I can't recognise.

With the sun burning red, the wise guide slips into the

alleyways, the tributaries feeding Ledras Street. Village is found in the city. There is much history to be found in, on, underneath these walls, this soil. Little details, silent clues, Lusignan, Roman, British Colonial, Greek, Ottoman, finding their way through concrete.

A beautiful breeze flows through the streets. With the sun-induced lethargy shaken off Ledra, its alleyways become alive with people, the lifeblood of any city. Eons ago, before the Atlantic Ocean flooded the Mediterranean Basin, Cyprus must have been the top of a mountain range, with Nicosia base camp to the summit, winds whistling through the rocks. These man-made peaks and valleys have a different sound now. Ancient historic buildings spill out onto the pavement. The jabber of imbibing humanity hits the ear, each voice wanting its own moment of love-angst-awe-anger-love to ricochet against the tight walls. Up, above the café clientele, are homes, and visible through the pale blue flaming slats of a window are faded family photographs arranged on a bare wall. No black, no white, just sepia. One is askew, trying to peer out of the window and see what the fuss is about. Do we too look back and yearn for that golden past, or has that past become muted to sepia forever for us?

Next to the café there is a wrought-iron fence and an entrance to the Church of Faneromeni, 'She Who Has Shown Herself' – the meaning of the name; and as soon as we crossed past the railings, she revealed her magic. Upon entering her courtyard all noise disappears and an almost holy, spiritual essence descends. You can virtually taste the calm, silent sanctity in the air, in your soul. I am almost tempted to pray. The acoustics and monumental architecture, not God, are the magic. If God were here I'd take him to court and sue him for abandoning his children, for man's inhumanity, and demand compensation for this hell of green lines. I do not judge anyone for their faith or for this soothing place with its offers of hope and peace. Leaving the sanctified silence and solitude of the courtyard, humanity's soundtrack switches back on with full force as we slip out of the alleys and back onto Ledras Street.

We walk back to the hotel. Thank you and goodnight to my guide. Thank you, Nicosia, for being my Faneromeni-Alley-Ledras Street magic. You are the way I've felt my whole life: one foot in the village, the other in the city.

Yours,
The Village Idiot

THE ENDLESS DAY

Dize Kükrer

There she was again. She had touched a wall in the Walled City. She recalls: 'It was not solid. I have the residue of mud on my hands.'

There was a silhouette at the far end of the room. The probability of it being a staged display of the unconscious mind bugged her; it could have been a product of her imagination. There was a black cat across the room. Rachel couldn't place herself in the room anyway, the silhouette and the cat could have been the same. She was never able to grasp the essence of perception. She just saw; her eyes were her sole witnesses. She looked at the surreal and dysfunctional scenery. There was barely any furniture in the room she was standing in. The cat could be any colour, but it appeared black in the darkness. The cat disappeared as Rachel followed it into the street. She didn't need any guidance, the road led her to the place she was supposed to be where truths are revealed and no statement could be contradictory.

For all she knew, what she witnessed was a display of Zach's sickening motives.

When she looked back at the image of the cat in her memory, she saw a reflection of her curiosity. She wanted to be truthful. She found herself in the abyss: 'Someone must have dreamt about me, I was the bearer of bad news'.

She knew that she was the subject in many stories, but Rachel would rather be her own object in inevitable discourses. She saw Zach standing at a doorway. She followed him through a narrow and musty corridor and up the stairs. He opened a door leading to his unfurnished apartment. In a room filled with second-hand books, Rachel spilled her heart out. Zach made the soup of words Rachel blurted out into stories with no end and no beginning. He twisted the words in his mouth so well that the rest of the room was helpless against the undertow of his imagination. 'A dark figure, possibly a man, stands on a porch overlooking a mass of evergreens. He whispers to the skies asking for deliverance from evil. His embodied soul is represented with black clothes, yellow teeth and rhetorical questions. He descends from the sky of a hectic week with no weekends and no rest. He carefully picks up words from contextual meanings and places them in the pointy thoughts of bleak lovers. His words scrape the skin, scrunch ribcages and blast the hearts of honey drippers and dishonest drapers. Eyes in sockets watch little annoyances in air pockets of the newly constructed malls. Consumers stain the walls of changing rooms with unmatched desires for designer clothes. In living rooms, the frenzy of information stirs up tension and animated mouths repeat the tales of the world.'

It was overwhelming. Rachel stepped back into the street and headed west. She looked up to the sky above and saw nothing but dark blue. She walked through a labyrinth of soft beige exteriors hiding exotic interiors. She got in her car that was parked in a narrow street by a mosque. The car was a mobile jukebox that contained boots and books. She grabbed a black box from the pile of pens and cables and rolled a cigarette. It was almost 9 o'clock. The authorities got carried away in foreign ideologies and set the clocks in such a way that they would no longer represent the time but mere hours and specific minutes of appointed obligations for family, work or leisure. People only were there and then, in between monochromatic planes of stocks and herds. Rachel drove past frameless displays of prosperity and abundance. The streets were illuminated only by shop signs. The road was uneven and so were the buildings. Rachel could not help but imagine the city a century ago. Was it any different? It was again the construct of a corrupt kind, the human kind. She kept on driving and, when she realised she didn't know where to go, she headed home.

Rachel's home could best be described as a pile of uncared-for objects. Rachel couldn't be bothered by principles of interior design, so she piled everything in one room. The rest of the rooms were empty. She knew her personality could be read by the arrangement of her house and she could not care less. She hung her bag on the rack by the entrance and walked past the kitchen into the living room. She sat on the lone whimsical chair facing a window. The window had a view of a pleasant square with poplar trees and Ottoman houses.

'However did it come to this?' she thought to herself. The Earth had almost finished another rotation around the sun, and everything was the same. She had gotten another diploma by the middle of the year and loved and lost several men in the second half. Yet everything felt the same. From where she sat, the end of the world was as close as the Big Bang. She sat there on that second-hand armchair, her gaze focused on the window. The window appeared in her dream a couple of nights ago. She stood by the window and had the feeling – the unstoppable urge – to jump off. She believed she could fly but the fear of falling paralysed her. She just stood there, watching the pedestrians passing by. The dream ended in hesitation, Rachel was hindered by her fears.

Words ideally represent interesting stories of each individual. Compositions of words are coherent with the picker's personality. Characters are read through the many meanings attached to single words. She was aware of this, yet she never hesitated, not with words. She was becoming his and hers; close as in proximity and common as in, well, as in commonality.

She walked out, again, this time towards the square. The night had begun and she couldn't keep herself enclosed within the walls of her house any longer. She found her friends at a table and exchanged looks with many beautiful sets of eyes. Zach's gaze upon her and the others reminded her of the cat. She was his prey. Evil within her made her not the hunted but the huntress. It was a waste of time.

She was convinced that if she took a pilgrimage out of the walled city she would be cleansed of all the lies and liars, all the deceivers and the deceit itself. She imagined herself before recorded history existed in the unobserved universe. She wondered who she would run to when she needed comfort; the liar, the deceiver or the deceit?

Zach was her poison and her antidote. Running away seemed like the better option.

She had her breakfast at the harbour frequented by barbaric sailors, her lunch in a faithful settlement of idolaters, and her dinner was served in a civilised environment, in another Walled City. She travelled the endless Road, between the unsuspecting meadows and the sea. The sun had risen before she fell asleep and fired up her thirst before she could reach her means. The sunset revealed an inexplicable beauty in silence on a hill overlooking ploughed soil of the island of love; once a goddess remembered for her beauty, now a whore. There she was again, as she breathed out her impurities to make room for endless possibilities.

When Rachel's displacement became a mere excuse of point-less escape, she found herself looking in the eyes of the deceiver again, in a square in the Walled City. Her eyes lacked emotion; she turned her back and left.

Rachel was sitting at a café in the heart of the Walled City. It was all dark and quiet except for a dozen chairs or more; paths led to the square, the one occupied by misfits. She had drunk more than she should have, every face and every word reminding her of someone else that she should have been. It was a hot summer day, she could no longer bear to sit in the same chair listening to the same words and looking at the same eyes. She decided to take a walk and left the heat where it belonged, on a rickety metal table decorated with all the condensed curiosity of glasses filled with intoxicants.

She walked through a street that used to be a vibrant shopping district, now in ruins. The mannequins stared blankly back at her as she walked by. The walled city was laid out as a labyrinth; those who had no idea where they were going were led by the city herself. She came by a crossroads. One of the paths led to a confused construct of religion. A pain-ridden melody of rock 'n' roll sounded from the bar across the street. She walked straight ahead, another crossroads interrupted her steps. She kept walking straight, she couldn't waste any time deciding on that hot summer night. Her judgement was impaired by all the things she put in her mouth and all those that came out of it. The street she walked ended at a gate. Her path was obstructed by a wide and tall iron gate with four narrow gaps at eye level. She wasn't able to take another step but she wanted to keep walking. She knocked on the door.

Footsteps sounded from the other side. She saw some silhouettes becoming faces and shoulders. She asked the men standing in the dark if they would let her in: 'I want to keep walking. Can you open the gate please?' They asked for her name, she didn't lie. The reason for their interest was obvious in their question. One of the men made a phone call. The doors opened before too long.

She was in.

There were three of them dressed in different uniforms, yet all were the same. One was dressed casually compared to the rest, he had a cotton cap on. The other one had a helmet on his head and a big gun in his hands.

She kept on walking. There was no time for details. One of the men caught up with her in the dark corridor that felt like a street that had lost its way a long time ago. She kept on walking the endless aisles of broken walls; a faint light made the ghostly ruins visible. It was all in black and white in that quarter of the city. No yellow sandstone walls were present, nor were there any green uniforms.

They stopped at another square with paths leading to at least four other streets. Rachel tried to walk away from the man; she walked through an opening that apparently used to be a door. It led to a young forest. After a couple of steps from the forest within the city, she came to another dead end.

'This is where the candy-striped blue volunteers are, you shouldn't go any further.'

'Would I be bothering them if I said hello?'

He was silent.

She said hello.

No one replied.

She was barely there, barren. She stripped down to her bones, she thought no one was able to see her anymore. Men with no sympathy roamed her naked streets. In the pitch-black blindness, she bruised her knees. The road suddenly stopped leading her. She was led into a zone where her body and soul were raped. All that went on in the streets was off the record; she didn't exist there. No one did.

The walled city was in suspense, stories stopped following plots, everything was stuck in reverse. In imposed beliefs of the soldier and his fulfilling weapons lay Rachel's desires. She wanted to roam the streets she wasn't allowed to see.

A door stood as an archway, open to a set of stairs. Now she was looking over the city from the fourth level. The man with her knew exactly what he was doing up on the roof. He was the one who opened the heavy iron doors and let her in. He tried to guide Rachel through the zone and not let go of her arm. Rachel couldn't stand authority, but she enjoyed domination. On the top of that forgotten building, Rachel watched the city with her drunken eyes. She felt his breath on her neck, his dick on her ass. She felt like the city herself – captured and held hostage. The city was held hostage by men with arms. They were protecting the land their ancestors had fought for. Their way of things didn't satisfy her, yet she was grateful for the fact that they were indeed protecting the soil. Men appointed to guard the gates weren't exactly aware of this; maybe they were, who knows. Their presence; the barbed wires they had weaved and the tall gates they had constructed, kept everyone out, everyone including the entrepreneurs who wanted to cover every inch of the soil for their benefit. The soil was nourishing. Rachel had contradictory feelings about this. She kept on thinking as she walked down the stairs. She tried to solve the riddle of the deceit. The way back to the gate, like a dream after being awoken, slipped through her eyelids. She was back on the other side of the gate.

Unable to see through all the fuss about conquerors and conquests, she sat on the same table. The crowd had dispersed. There were several people left who were curious, almost worried, about the whereabouts of Rachel. She couldn't explain cohesively but blurted out some words: '100 miles away. Serene. Serenity. A long-lost encounter with a friend.'

Someone asked 'Who? Where?'

'... I just don't understand why I was looking for it.' Rachel continued, 'Reminiscing, reliving a romanticised past. It is hunger. It is now or never. It's hung in the air over the city. Sun-kissed memories of a meadow in the afternoon, on the way to church. I had a sudden loss of balance. I took a leap and fell on my back, amongst the purple, red and yellow spring blossoms.'

LEDRA

Norbert Bugeja

Translated by Irene Mangion

On Ledra Street, your body calls to me:
teasing, it draws out this short parade
to the wind's limits, where my soul
set aside slivers of gold
I never knew it had,
until she found them.
On the olive-strewn path
young cats taunt the soldiers,
skipping from one story to the other
until it's time for us to embark
on our silent walk to Phaneromeni:
here, where the tears of the ancient city
gather in islands under flaring skirts,
where creaseless looks reveal
modern museums to an extinct god.

Across the road, your body calls to me.
In my chest, the heavy steps of lahmajoun.

THE LANGUAGE OF
THE DEAD ZONE

Yiannis Papadakis

The accusation of treachery was not the only thing we had in common. We also shared a speech impediment. We stuttered.

Being inside the Dead Zone was a kind of internal exile. People found themselves in a place that belonged to neither, estranged from their own people, outsiders treated with suspicion. When it came to the language of the Dead Zone, the exile was triple.

First, we were exiled from both our native tongues, Greek and Turkish, neither of which could provide a common medium of communication there. Even within the 'native tongue' we were already in exile. Our native tongue was neither the standard Greek nor the standard Turkish that we had learned at school, but our own dialects. When one tried to talk, the 'standard' language did not seem so standard after all. The standard languages were created by Turkey and Greece by expunging 'foreign' words, as 'foreign people' were exiled in the bosoms of the mother-fatherlands. Speaking the 'standard language' in Cyprus was arduous. Unlike the dialects that flowed easily, talking in the standard languages required effort, and led to stuttering. Many people in Cyprus had been bilingual, or rather bi-dialectal. As animosity grew and people were separated, as people were learning to talk like true Turks and Greeks, as the other dialect was becoming that of the enemy and fines were imposed for using it, we were left with no language in common. Except that provided by our common colonial past and desire to be western: English. That was the second exile. We discussed the Cyprus Problem in English.

Talking about the Cyprus Problem was also separated by the Dead Zone. Our heroes, their murderers; our rights, their wrongs; our history, their mythology; our Happy Peace Operation, their barbaric Turkish invasion; our state, their so-called state. It was so easy to talk in the official idiom. Words, thoughts and arguments flowed because they were already out there, ready-made, used all the time. One had to invent from scratch a language to talk about Cyprus as a whole, one that both could use: a language of understanding, empathy, and forgiveness. It was one that had to be invented as people hesitantly tried to talk to each other inside the Dead Zone. This was a language of uncertainty and questioning, not one composed of readily found, capitalised, sacred truths. When people tried to talk there, they often stuttered.

This difficulty emerged even when trying to talk of a basic human experience like pain. The language of pain had been hijacked by the two officialdoms' politics. The language of politics in Cyprus had been turned into a language of pain and suffering by both sides, but in a way that never allowed consideration of the other's pain. Both sides were screaming with pain, with true pain, even the same kinds of pain. They were locked in a perverse screaming match to make one's pain heard over the other's. Peace activists inside the Dead Zone even had trouble talking about peace. The word 'peace' had been torn apart. The language of peace had been hijacked with talk of the 'Happy Peace Operation' and 'peaceful coexistence'; talk of peace used to deny others' pain and hide one's own violence.

The language of pain was the only one allowed in Cyprus to talk about Cyprus. Actually, only the language of the pain of Cyprus was taken seriously. Other problems elsewhere received scant attention. The same took place within. Only the Cyprus Problem counted as a real problem worth talking about. Everything else was minor; it could wait. Problems of discrimination against migrants, religious minorities or women, were waved away. If anyone dared breach the silence, one was accused of – what else? – treachery. 'How dare you accuse us of violating human rights when we accuse the other side of this?' The Cyprus Problem became the perfect alibi for abuses within. And talk about the Cyprus Problem always had to be in tears. Smirking, let alone laughing at us, was a highly improper manner of conduct.

Another reason why the people of the Dead Zone stuttered was the constant fear of moving a bit too close to the other side; the fear of saying something that someone would report back to their own side, where they would be publicly condemned as traitors. To speak there was a dangerous tightrope: a scary experience for which none of us had practised. It could only be learnt on the spot during the performance, inside the Dead Zone.

NICOSIA

Gür Genç

Translated by Aydın Mehmet Ali

You fooled me into stay-ings on your side, Nicosia ...
    In your divided backyards, under revered date palms
I got hooked on the secret hash along with those with broken
    tongues
    In place of a home I slept and awoke in the Armenian grave-
    yard
the very same, Isabel d'Ibelini in my dreams
    I traded my pride
for a metal bed of springs and a hand-me-down 28-inch bicycle-
    skeleton
chucked out by the shut-down bordello
    Even though the elders may still smell the scent of jasmine, I
only inhaled the militarist stench of sweat and wounds,
in your streets
    On your stinking streams, if I were to land a heron
fairer than your young spinsters, V-necked,
I wasn't able to

You've held my name in your mouth for far too long spit it out
    now, Nicosia ...

HOT CITY DREAM

Zoe Piponides

Skirting around in the open,
I walk away from circular words,
parallel lines that steer aside
the central nerve whereby
a city's soul might rest.

Skirting around in the open,
in hot still air fans whir awake,
a silent river gushes fresh, lungs
swell, reach the water's edge,
the scent of rain-soaked earth.

Skirting around in the open,
beside those arrowhead walls
are stalls of lahmacun and olive pie,
vines with red-veined leaves
held eye to eye.

Skirting around in the open,
hot city snaps up rows of sacks
for flour and spice, turns
them into trays of baklava -
prepares to share out diamonds.

COCCINELLA, OR BEYOND DATA

Maria Petrides

The mile is smooth like the Ionian sky,
turquoise and feathery as the wind whistles,
echoes spring from the searing seawater.
From there to here, a cornering line of British barbed wire
bears vestiges of the perforated Ermou caddesi.
From UN wire to unwiring this naturalised protection at any rate
between mili(tarrying) jets flying low
and moderate alerts lying on car windows
autographed by the authorities of Akrotiri.
'Do not leave your personal belongings unattended.'
I smile, glassy-eyed,
airport and subway announcements post 9/11
interpose my freedom to choose how I perceive,
'if you see something, say something'.
Where am I. Traversing the caveat of
New York, the Kingdom, and Cyprus.
What is imminent in every short moment,
which terrorist, thief or muscle?
It breezed from the west.
In a flickering movement beyond,
a twinkling vagary emanates
from an azure at hand.
I smile again, a single smile this time.
She flaps her wings as I hum
'ladybird ladybird fly away',
and she heads farther west to that base.

KNIT

Christos Tsiailis

On a fine Wednesday afternoon, the citizens of Nicosia, a small city on an island in the Mediterranean Sea, started a campaign to bring down all hospitals, clinics and pharmacies.

The Mayor of the city was informed of the situation only after his secretary told him that there were people out in the streets with tools. He looked down from his window and indeed he saw pedestrians on their way to the Eastern suburbs of the city, where the General Hospital was, holding shovels, axes, hammers and whatever else they had found in their small yards.

He had had no idea what was going to happen that day. It was a paralysed city and he was the Mayor. He could not accept such a disgrace. What if the Media turned against him for loss of control? What if he became a figure of ridicule around the world? He got furious, and lost his temper. He called the Chief Inspector, but he was not in his office and he would not answer his phone. He became desperate. He called the President, some ministers, nobody was answering. He felt alone in this, for the first time in his career.

Three kilometres away from the Town Hall, at the General Hospital, the disillusioned people, driven by this strange desire, had already started hitting the cement walls.

The Mayor ran out of his office to ask for more details but his secretary was not in her office. Nobody was at Town Hall.

As soon as he got out he saw them; walking across Liberty Square as though it were a great battlefield and they were preparing for attack against an invisible foe. He thought suddenly of the Third Reich and its blind obedience to a leader. However here, nobody was talking to the people. It seemed to him that some collective subconscious directive, beyond any humour power, was controlling them.

And what was with the tools? he thought, while he moved next to the speechless sleepwalkers. His wife was there, walking gracefully in her high heels, holding the heavy pickaxe their gardener had recently bought. Their daughter was also there, he saw her further to the front as he ran in parallel to the queues, in an effort to reach the head of the body to see if there were a leader, after all.

As he ran, he spoke to nobody. He was not afraid of the metal in their hands. He was terrified of their silence and fixed stares.

Was it possible that this had to do with all those thousands of letters of complaint he had received in the past few months about roots under peoples' gardens? He remembered that almost all houses had reported this anomaly; even flat residents had called or sent letters about strange red roots that had climbed through their pipes and had been trying to choke their potted plants. The city had turned yellow with dying plants everywhere.

He ran through the park to reach the other side. All the pine trees were almost dead; the strange red roots were suffocating them. Suddenly he realised that the roots were not motionless. They were expanding in a slow rhythm, but not too slowly – he could catch the movement if he paid attention. He stood on the paved path and looked to his right and left. All the roots were moving to the centre of the city, towards Liberty Square, swirling like giant worms, slowly but effectively. Their movement was successful as the roots were thickening and creating strange geometrical shapes, as if they were knitting something. He looked back. In the far distance, behind the buildings, he saw it.

Three days before, the whole population of the city had surrounded the Venetian Walls, on top of the eleven bastions. They were holding bags with medicines from the hospitals and pharmacies. They had looted every single ward and storage room and taken everything.

Masses of roots had gathered in the eleven moats and were trying to puncture the walls to enter the old city. With the instructions of the doctors and the nurses from all the clinics, the pharmacies and the General Hospital, the people were administering the drugs in order. First, they opened all the antibiotics and smeared them on the roots inside the moats. When a thick, yellow mist started coming out of the moats and the roots stopped moving, the people cheered and shouted in triumph. But then, suddenly, the roots started swelling. Everyone feared that if they were not about to burst, they were definitely getting stronger. The thickest roots stood upright. At that moment, the Doctor in charge ordered everybody who held tranquilisers and local anaesthetics to inject. They had to sedate the wrath of this strange beast before it attacked. They thrust everything they had into the roots – barbiturates, benzodiazepines, halothane, nitrous oxide and morphine.

The swelling of the roots indeed was compromised. They became smaller, shorter, fast as the pools of sedatives were absorbed by the red flesh. A red, thick, squeezed-to-the-ground carpet was now the surface along the bottom and sides of the moats. The people stayed there and waited. Unsure. Not yet relieved. The roots were not dead.

After a minute of dead silence, the yellow mist around the Venetian walls became red and much thicker. A red cloud covered the town in seconds. It was pollen. First, it entered the nostrils of everybody standing around there. They all stood still. Idle. Hypnotised, they watched the red pollen head to the centre of the Old City. A small plant started growing there, next to Omerye Hamam, right in the centre. It was a Judas tree and it started growing fast, fed by the pollen. Within a few hours, it grew so high that the buildings had already started looking puny next to it. It grew flowers, millions of flowers. It was a wonderful tree.

A strange magnetic power was slowly consuming the people's will. A few of them managed to take a few steps towards the tree and attacked the pollen with more inhalational anaesthetics, with halothane and desflurane, and they threw litres of analgesics like hydrocodone and paracetamol in the water pipes and the sewers to inflict a blast to the tree directly, but the tree withstood their attack.

It was then that the roots breached the moat and started building the foundations of the Great Cube around the Judas Tree. The designs of the roots as they knitted their way up were out of this world. The roots had a special kind of ingenuity, an ancient wisdom such that they designed intelligent lines on top of lines of hieroglyphics, as if they were writing a book no human could read.

Right there and then, everybody – every single citizen – lost consciousness.

The order to destroy all hospitals, clinics and pharmacies became the only directive in their minds. The Judas Tree and the Cube were fighting back.

What the Mayor saw caused him to stand motionless for a full minute. Right in the centre of Nicosia, inside the Venetian walls, one and a half kilometres from the periphery of the old town, he had a perfect view of the huge cube constructed by the roots.

'They are aliens. And they kept me oblivious all these days', thought the Mayor to himself. 'Why did I stay in my office for two months ignoring the desperate calls from my wife and daughter?'

He started running, trying to avoid any contact with the roots.

He knew he had to find someone to help him. If he stayed here alone and allowed the roots to complete the cube, they would be finished.

The Mayor found no one. He thought of his wife and daughter. Why was he away from them? He wanted to grab a tool and join the march. He touched the roots and inhaled the air near them. But the roots and the mist would not affect him. He cut a piece from a root and bit it. Nothing. To his dismay, he was immune. It was his worst nightmare. There he was, all alone, and he had to fight for his City, the city he so much loved.

He ran back towards the Old City. He passed the walls and reached the giant cube. He stood one hundred metres away from it to have a general view. He suddenly realised that there was no ground under his feet. Only red roots, moving slowly, dragging him closer, bringing him metres away from the cube. As he went close enough to touch its sides, already knowing he could not be harmed by the roots, through the holes of the knitted designs, he saw the magnificent tree. Its trunk, about sixty metres in diameter, had destroyed many buildings around it. It was over four hundred metres tall already – and still it kept growing.

The Mayor was desperate to reach its centre, but there was not a single hole that he could fit through. In a last effort, he started climbing the hieroglyphics. He grabbed the thin lines of root ends that had crafted the wonderful 'small letters' of the strange language – punctuation and all. The cube did not fight back. Perhaps this was the way in. No communication between the city leader and the tree that claimed the city, just the climbing of a book he would never read.

The entire city was now assembled in front of the clinics and the hospital. They broke down the entrances and began to hack at the walls, floors, roofs and basements. The thick walls of the buildings began to weaken as the people damaged the iron structures inside the walls. Huge chunks of cement started falling. People were dying, but they did not know any pain. Like termites eating their way through, they laid siege to the hospital.

The Mayor reached the top of the cube. The hole in the centre was now only two metres wide and the roots were weaving fast, closing it.

The Mayor jumped down blindly. As he fell, he hit thick branches, and giant flowers fell with him. The longer he fell, the more he realised it was a nonstop descent. He was in another dimension. He used all the concentration he had to snatch onto a branch. He managed to stabilise his body. He had to go down, and the only way was near the trunk, but the more he tried to slide towards it, the more the branch extended outwards. A strange force was pushing him to turn his body to the cube and look at the inside of its walls. The light of the ambient Nicosia sun was coming in waves from the designs. He gazed more carefully. And there it was. The designs that had seemed like hieroglyphics to the outside, formed letters inside. Letters that formed words, words that formed sentences, paragraphs from the top of the cube down to its bottom. It was a huge text.

It took him no more than two paragraphs to understand that he was reading a book from some kind of a Bible. The language was ancient Greek, of a version of John's *Apocalypse*. A twisted one, very different from the one he remembered, without Angels of Doom, or Knights on Horses.

He stood on the branch.

'Show yourself.' he shouted.

He looked down. Suddenly he realised that he was not far from the ground. It was not a bottomless cube after all. Beneath him, hundreds of metres down, he saw a normal Nicosia. The ordinary streets with the hustle and bustle, the cars commuting to their usual destinations, people at work, and out shopping. He was looking at Nicosia in all its grandeur, but with an awkward change. There were no hospitals, clinics or pharmacies. It was an alternate reality inside the cube. A better one.

Instinctively he looked up on the higher branches. He was not alone. There were many more people sitting on the branches. All this time he had thought he was fighting for his city alone, but he had been mistaken. Everybody had thought so; every citizen of this city had assumed a fallacious individuality against a crowd of hypnotised people with garden tools. They were all sitting there on the branches, looking at their happier self, the better one down there. He saw his wife, he saw the President on a nearby branch, he saw his daughter sitting further up, he saw doctors, and nurses.

This was hell and down there was heaven.

He called his wife and daughter's names, but they did not hear him. As he tried in vain to move to a higher branch, he felt his mobile in his pocket. He pulled it out. As soon as he turned it on, Facebook notifications started coming through. Notifications from the past three months. The last one was a 'like' from his daughter, on a photo of himself he'd posted only five minutes ago, as though nothing had happened that day outside the cube.

He shouted for the last time: 'If I am outside right now, and I am also here, and if I am down there, too, and if this is Apocalypse, then who am I?'

His phone rang with an unfamiliar tone.

WITHIN THE WALLS

Marilena Zackheos

I am granted permission
to step right in. She motions
'This is my palace; my Sarayonu'.

She is forgetting.
I forget too, momentarily.

This home is not stately.
Sky starred
with blank bullets –
kittens littering streets like vermin.

Courting strangers
in Sarayonu Square
and I, a paper cut-out
in this place:

reciting words of empire
– meaningless between us –
its insignia before us
on the courthouse yellow-stone.

She tugs at the sleeve of my sweater.
'Your Majesty, forgive me but tonight
I am no decent play-date'.

As in all encounters,
we will search high and low
for sympathy in each other.

In the giving of the hand,
the wearing of a smile,
that genteel inclination of the head –
our practised intimacies.

In her mini hand in mine,
intramural
flesh
to activate.

BUZZING BEES IN MY HOUSE

Münevver Özgür Özersay

I come home. You are sitting in an armchair reading, holding a book or a newspaper. Or you are learning Greek, with headphones in your ears. Or you are listening to Shakespeare on audio, or the news. At home, in the garden, on the road, you are always listening to the radio. The radio is constantly talking. The TV is consistently talking. It talks in Turkish. In English. In Greek. You listen to what is being said and the more you listen, the more you talk. The more you read, the more you write. The more you write, the more you read.

Words, words, words... Words buzzing like bees, words filling up every corner of our house.

Every time I return home, I am confused. Our rooms seem to be filling up with these buzzing words. Lunch time: in our house, that's time for the 'news'. Anxious words, angry words, breaking statements spew forth from the speakers, scatter around, hit the walls, bounce off the ceiling, an army. They create a ball. As their humming increases we are silenced. The humming. The radio is announcing important news. We are all ears! Silently we eat our lunch.

Sometimes, along with important news, we have important guests. My father's guests ... Important issues are being discussed with important guests. My mother listens attentively. If our guests are English-speaking, my mother is speechless in two languages; listening in only one. We, the children, are always silent, so that our kitchen can better hear the important words of the important issues. Even our dining table, chairs and cutlery on crockery fall silent.

I do not understand what they are talking about most of the time. Our talk around the table is just like the old Turkish prayers we were forced to memorise without understanding at elementary school. The words have not changed. Imperialism, mimperialism ... Bees, buzzing bees ... Bees like members of a secret sect, hiding in a beehive ... Capitalists, workers, labourers ... What is the meaning of republican? What does communal mean? Who are the leftists? Why are they calling my father a 'traitor'? Who are the exploiters? Who are the exploited? Where am I located within all this? Am I a capitalist or a worker? To which class do children belong?

Mum, where are you in all this?

I come home. You are knitting, needles and threads in hand; you are sitting on the sofa, holding your wool. Or you are crocheting. Just like that, always, with something in your hands, you are sitting and knitting. After chemotherapy, your hands and feet ache. Your wrists ache. You do not say anything. The TV is talking. TV is constantly talking. Are you listening to what is being said Mum? Or is the TV shouting to hide your silence? You are covering up, Mum! You are constantly knitting covers!

I come home. To our home in the North of a still divided Nicosia. In front of the cooker, you are cooking something. Your back turned to me; you are occupied with something. You are occupied both with the food and me. You say, 'You are anaemic again. You look really pale. You are not taking good care of yourself.' Food is bubbling in the saucepan. Hot steam rises, lapping the kitchen walls. My father is not there. No bees. No loneliness in the middle of the crowd. No humming silence. I come home. In front of the kitchen sink you are doing the washing up. Cold water is flowing down your hands. The plates rattle. Your back turned towards me, you are angry: 'You are like a closed box, you never share anything!' you say. Yes, it's true. You are so right. I really don't share anything. Like a shadow, I slip under the door and run away.

Later, we sit and silently eat our food. No radio news. No guests. My aunties invite us over for coffee. And then suddenly, one day, all the threads and stiches tied off, all the knitting is knitted, all food cooked, dishes washed. You also finish. We are at the hospital in the South of Nicosia. Your whole body is covered in cancer cells, your whole body your unspoken words. The doctors say, 'You can take your mother home, somewhere close to her family'. A strangled cry in protest of the silence wants to jump out of my throat. I do not let it. The ambulance arrives. Screaming, it moves through the streets. Screaming, we cross the border.

I sit in the living room with my laptop on my knees. My little daughter sings at the top of her voice and dances around me. Then, she runs towards me all excited. She points to the computer and with self-confidence orders: 'Pick me up, Mum!'

I sit on the couch in our living room. My earphones are in my ears and I am listening to 'Nazım Oratorio' by Fazıl Say. In my imagination I hang all that my parents put between me and what they call society on barbed wire. Tears hide in the corner of my eyes and still listening to my father, I keep silent.

My eldest daughter comes through the door. I turn to look at her. She never talks. She never shares anything with me. She looks so pale and I am concerned that she is not taking care of herself.

'What are you doing?' she asks.

I say 'Nothing'. She perches on the couch next to me. She plays with her mobile. For some time, we sit like that. Then, she turns her back, slips away under the door just like a silent shadow, and goes to her room.

TWO SYLLABLES, SIX LETTERS

Anthony Anaxagorou

'It's better to not go back to the village,
the subverted paradise silent
in the shatter of shrapnel'
Ramon Lopez Velarde

Two syllables,
six letters
nailed to the sea.

An island at ease with running waves,

I climb the smell of its earth,
thirsty with olive trees, monasteries
beguiling an unsatisfied god.

Trekking deeper, past orange groves,
hacked meats and leaking salads
where a constellation of stones hurt history.

What I find weighs like a scab
on the back of a donkey
dwelling in dystrophy;
who took the strain of injustice,
whose hooves bled while the upright
harnessed every horizon but his.

The liberals and philanthropists
corked volcanos, blocked the stampede
of empire, of colonialism & genocide,
but the donkey,

the one who dreamt of a clean moon
became too attached to blood:
his journey laden with misfortune
but he went on.

United with his brothers, his sisters,
even as the winter rains forgot to wet
the edge of the Levant's heart,
the summer sun forgot to shine
turning instead to burn a wind
containing the stench of a burnt village,

still
he went on.

His island's pyrite
bared like the earth's entrails.
Wine dripping from wooden tables.
Blood dripping from wooden tables
and everywhere was ending.

But that was then
in a time when donkeys were killed
for grieving, when the pestilence came to test shores,
pride and character.

They would rather we forget
but over in the villages,
a few who fought to return what was –
a peace,
who sang the song of an island

two syllables
six letters
nailed to the sea.

ISLAND IN THE SUN

Melissa Hekkers

'There! This is the place!' points Max, pulling out an advertising leaflet from his back pocket.

We both stood at the heart of the busy Solomou Square, having just got off the bus.

'Can you see? This is the leaflet the agent showed me back in Cameroon. He told me this was the backyard of the college campus in Nicosia.'

Dumbfounded, I was looking down at the Tripoli Park within the moat of the old town. I cringed as I acknowledged the tactics used to lure migrants into coming to the island, not just to study, but to accommodate the jobs that locals don't want to indulge in or don't have the time for. Who wouldn't want to own the up-bringing of their children?

Max brings me back to the present, pulling me onwards through the crowd. He wants to show me how he spends his days as he awaits his pending application for asylum.

I want to justify Cyprus's stance towards opening its doors to migrants back in the late 80s. Locally there was a gap in the economy, and before the financial meltdown a couple of years ago the island was prospering and could afford the helping hand of foreign nationals. Amongst the daunting stories about the manner in which migrants are treated on the island, there were some positive ones. I wanted Max to meet Lillie, who for the past fourteen years has made Nicosia her home. Now, when she goes back to the Philippines, she feels like a stranger there. If she could bring her nuclear family to Cyprus, she would make it her home indefinitely.

But I also know why Max left his country in pursuit of a better life, and how that dream was shattered when he began to experience what it means to migrate to an island where migration policies fluctuate insistently.

When I first met Max, he had just been told that the local college he had paid a substantial amount of money to register for before he left his home country was a fraud. That the promise that, once in Cyprus, he could travel to other European countries during academic breaks was a lie, and that he wasn't, after all, allowed to work as a student. He still had to pay his rent, and working illegally was his only option to get by.

'This is where Marichelle used to work. By work, you know what I mean,' Max tells me as we pass a dubious night bar off Rigainis Street. It's daytime, and that awkward silence lurks outside these locales, an ambiguous silence of what happens behind doors in the later hours of the evening.

Marichelle paid six thousand US dollars to an agent in Nepal who had offered her a job working as a waitress in a restaurant. I hear her soft-spoken voice telling me '... but *he* did not tell me that he would bring me somewhere where people would come to make love with me. He didn't tell me that, because if he tell me something like that, I don't follow him.'

Like many others who have been smuggled onto the island, they envision that through building a new life in Europe, they will be 'accepted', they will be somewhat relieved of the life they leave behind. 'I will have a new life, people will not judge me; will not treat me like I am monster', Marichelle had explained.

'Have you heard Marichelle speak Greek? I've been here a lot longer than her but I don't speak Greek like her!' smiles Max. We've almost reached the Saint Joseph's Convent where we're meeting Ayline, but we sit on the steps outside the Phaneromeni School to wait for a while.

'You know, there's a legend about this place,' I say, looking towards the Ayia Tsambika Church to our left. 'It's said that in the medieval times there used to be an underground tunnel that the ladies of the Louisignan Palace near Ayia Sofia used to make their way over here so that they wouldn't be seen,' I tell Max.

He looks out towards the north. He doesn't say anything for a while until, looking down at his feet and cell phone, he confides quietly, 'I wish there was a tunnel I could just disappear through. That's honestly how I felt when I was detained in Menoyia for nine months when I was caught working.'

Max lifts his head up. Eyes closed, he really begins to speak. 'In Menoyia it's more like torture. You know, there was a doctor there. You have a headache it's panadol, you have a tooth ache it's panadol, you have stomach problem, you have a sore leg or anything, everything is panadol, there was no other medicine, just panadol and vitamins ... So every time you get sick you have to write a letter saying you want to see the doctor and when you go to the doctor he will just give you Panadol. This was the only treatment they give in the prison. And the food wasn't enough, it wasn't okay. They would call us names like Mavro, poushto Mavro, it means gay black, poushto mavro, pezevengki.'

I've heard these name-callings on so many occasions. I don't know what to say, except to comfort him and remind him that he's out now, it's behind him.

'Yeah, I know. But who do you trust?' he asks me. He now knows Cyprus won't be his home for much longer. 'It was difficult to trust a lawyer, or pay money, people lost too much money in that prison. These were the challenges we were facing every day, and the worst part of it was you were in prison. You don't know your sentence, there's no time limit, you can be there for one month, you can be there for two months or a year or two years, there's no time limit, only on paper does it say that in some cases you can stay there for six months but after that they have to let you out.'

'You can trust me,' I say as I stand up ready to make a move. 'Come, let's go,' I gesture, I want to change the heavy tone, I want to take away the burden he and so many others carry on their journey here.

I know Ayline can turn this around. She's a mother figure to so many migrants in Nicosia. I sometimes feel that my privilege as an EU citizen cannot match my compassion, that speaking on my own behalf just isn't enough. I want Max to find his voice and the means to express himself. I want Marichelle to return to her parents and recover from her wounds after having been trafficked and sexually assaulted. I want Ashank to see his daughter once again, after eleven years apart. I want Kim to be allowed to make Nicosia her home, for she has no one and nowhere else to turn to.

We carry on walking. We pass the Arab quarters, acquainted with barbers and halal meat stores. I keep pace but Max stops outside his local store, where he and his friends spend most of their money buying countless phone cards to call home or address local authorities. If phones could talk, I think to myself. Only then would I truly know what really goes through Max's mind.

Turning to face the other side of the street we're standing on, I realise we're standing outside one of the only places Max feels at home, the only place perhaps where he can be himself. Standing outside the entrance of the old apartment building, this is the place where he celebrated his 26th birthday a couple of months ago. There's no one in right now as it's only used on Sundays. Each of them – or those who can pay thirty euros a month each – rent an apartment for just one day a week. But they make the most of it, often leaving the premises at 5am to get to work on Monday morning. It's where they rest, eat together, laugh. It's also were they wait.

'It's where we're family', Pina would agree, a young Vietnamese who fled from her employer in Limassol. 'He didn't treat me as a family, because if he treated me as a family he will not have said all these things to me, he said to me: I like you, I want you to come in my bed, like this, I told him I don't like because I'm a married woman, I have children in Vietnam', she had once told me. It was also Pina who envisioned making a house for poor children in the future. 'I want to take these children from the road, or people who have nothing to eat, who have no clothes. I want to help them. If god helps me, I will do this. This is my promise. Because I know how it feels. I don't know what a mother and father love is like. I still want that, but how do I get that, I lost everything.'

Outside the St Joseph's Convent, Ayline comes out to meet us holding her cell phone in hand, the only means of communication she has to talk to her two children. She's been the coach of Survivor Volleyball team, a club that comprises young Filipina, for the past twelve years. I realise that we're heading to the volleyball court, which lies behind the municipal swimming pool.

Having made it to the league of the Filipina Volleyball Tournament in Nicosia, they were the champions of the junior team in 2015 and runner up in the senior's category in 2016. The team has expanded and now has women from Sri Lanka, India and Bangladesh playing for them.

'It's better because we can get to know other nationalities, not only Filipinos, we can know them as well and not only see them walking and we can get to know their past', Ayline tells me with pride.

'With the team it's very important to have a good relationship out of court and in the court, it's not just go there and play. You also have to have an out of court relationship. So everybody is very close to me I would say, whenever there is a problem among the group, I will know.'

This is so different from the atmosphere in Kofinou, reflects Max. 'We live in containers there. There's four of us crammed in the rooms. It's okay for people like us who don't have anything, at least you have a roof over your head and it's a container, and then they have an AC but they control the AC. We don't have remotes.'

Seeing the camaraderie of all the ladies dressed in their volleyball kits, I doubt if any of their employers know anything about this opportunity for them to celebrate a sport they played back home. Panayiotis, a customs agent in the old town, surely knows: he sponsors their participation in the championship.

Agents start the whole process by preparing job descriptions. 'They will search through their database what ladies are suitable for this job. They will tell them that we have this job for you in Cyprus. If they accept they will sign, then we prepare the paper work. Sometimes there are Skype interviews, sometimes there are phone interviews, we're just trying to minimize the risk because when you join two people there's always a risk,' were Andrea's words. 'Cypriots are so demanding. By the end you have spoiled your relationship with them. I'm trying to avoid that risk because it's a big risk and as an employment agency it might be bad but I don't want to get involved in that.'

It's getting late and I want to make my way home. Max offers to walk me back to my car. We pass a firm spread of tagging on the back walls of the Municipal Arts Centre on our way.

'Refugees Welcome', it reads.

What about migrants, though?

At Famagusta Gate it's time to part. We say goodbye with a mutual understanding that we may never see each other again. His status is so ambiguous, he may be waiting here for an answer for the next six months. Or he may leave tomorrow.

Driving off, I imagine the stance of Famagusta Gate during Venetian rule. Then, the gates would open to the general public with the sunrise and close when the sun went down. Whether you made it in or out of the walled city very much depended on timing, status, social class, occupation. Nationality. Perhaps.

I TOO SHALL ANOINT THE STONES

Shola Balogun

It is said that a depressed man,
Fleeing from his homeland,
Lonely in the Eastern night,
Gathered the stones on his path
And made them his pillows,
And seeing the ladder
To the gate of heaven,
He trembled at the mystery of God
And anointed the stones.
I am a depressed man too,
Leaving behind my fathers' walls
Destitute in the African night.
I keep the stones in my hand
And count them along in every step.
I see the barbed wire
Rising on the high gates
Of the despots and tremble
At the misery of the helpless.

NICOSIA'S AFRICAN DIASPORA

Tinashe Mushakavanhu

For decades after independence, the Zimbabwe Warriors were perennial underachievers, the 'nearly-men' of African soccer, in spite of Peter Ndlovu, the team's captain and talisman, who was one of the longest-serving players in the history of professional English football ever since he had dazzled defences as a teen prodigy at Coventry City FC. In 2004, the jinx was broken when the team qualified for the Africa Cup of Nations for the first time. Among the history-makers was a contingent of 'foreign-based players' plying their trade in Cyprus, an unusual soccer destination. Cyprus became a national curiosity regularly mentioned on TV and radio sports broadcasts in Zimbabwe. Soccer made Cyprus glamorous; its fractious history remained unknown to many. It was just another overseas base for our soccer stars. As a former British colony, the Zimbabwean experience of the world has often been limited to the mother country and its commonwealth territories.

A wave of migrations to Cyprus became discernible in the mid-noughties. In a world in which soccer stars now influence lifestyles and culture, it is a matter of conjecture if they played a part inspiring this migratory pattern. The Zimbabwean government, under the direction of former ruler Robert Mugabe, made political decisions that resulted in record hyperinflation, the near total collapse of the economy and a massive humanitarian crisis, with seven million people on food aid and a third of the population migrating to other countries, mainly Australia, Britain, South Africa and the United States. Interest in other places was piqued when people failed to secure visas to their chosen destinations. Cyprus emerged as a favoured University Island. Its attractiveness was a consolation, mostly because of its proximity to continental Europe. Almost-Europe was good enough.

Before Nigerian author Chigozie Obioma wrote his critically acclaimed debut novel *The Fishermen*, he spent many years living in Cyprus. He wrote that even though Cyprus 'was not Europe; was not America; was not Asia; was not even Turkey ... Northern Cyprus is a nation in Europe for which no visa was required, that it is safe.' His second book, *An Orchestra of Minorities*, expresses the disappointment of arriving and discovering the Cypriot dream is not what he expected. He writes, "I pay, pay, pay to come here and then what did I discover? Africa in Europe."

Cyprus is still an enchanting island, steeped in myth and romance, a romance that goes back thousands of years, and it is astonishing to think that memory considers the black African experience in Cyprus a recent phenomenon. The historical amnesia is staggering. Kate Lowe, in *Black Africans in Renaissance Europe* argues that this perceived invisibility lies elsewhere, in the realities of national politics, in the still evolving effects of European colonisation and in the straitjacket of fashionable or acceptable historical scholarship. The long history of black settlement in many parts of Europe was denied for political and racial reasons, and the topic was successfully buried until the end of the twentieth century.

The island of Cyprus was on the black slave trade route. There was a dynamic slave market in Nicosia near the animal market, which was the usual place for them. Until the early twentieth century the animal market in Nicosia was set up in Sarayönü Square, now re-named Atatürk Square. If they were not slaves, black people in Nicosia worked as craftsmen, domestic servants or in trade. There were more women than men. Most of them lived in Lefkoşa, modern day Nicosia. What happened to these people over time? There is a yawning gap in historical scholarship, though Lowe provides a helpful explanation that 'arrival in Europe as slaves meant the systemic erasure of all the more significant aspects of their past, starting with their names, their languages, their religions, their families and communities, and their cultural practices.

Not finding answers to my questions in books or archives, I decided to talk to a cousin living in Nicosia, who is among the thousands lured there by Cypriot education. I wanted to learn from the details of his day-to-day existence and experiences in Nicosia, as part of the contemporary African diaspora. Moving to another country is not easy. When I was twenty-three, I left Africa for the first time to live and study in a small Welsh village. My knowledge of the 'diaspora' had been learnt second-hand, as no one in my family had been to Europe. It was at a time when the Internet was not as ubiquitous. I was curious about what my cousin knew about Cyprus before he went there.

'I didn't know much about the history and division of Cyprus when I decided to come here,' he said. 'I only knew that it was an island located in the eastern Mediterranean with a population of about 300,000 people, a Muslim country, and that Turkish was the official language.'

I did not react to his description of only half of the island.

What was his journey like and his arrival in Cyprus? I wondered, thinking of the journeys I had made myself, the arrivals that always arouse mixed feelings. 'Were you shocked or surprised when you arrived?' I asked. 'Did you have a sense of *déjà vu*? Did you immediately feel at home?'

'It was a shocking experience,' he said. 'When I arrived at the airport and wanted to talk to an immigration official, there was a huge language barrier because he couldn't speak English. I naively assumed English was the common language everywhere, but I was wrong. And the school representative who was responsible for picking me up from the airport just showed me where the school bus was parked and didn't explain anything to me.

'It was a strange welcome. I had to find out things on my own from the word go. Another shock was that the bus driver just dropped us at the school and drove off. I stood there stranded with my bags, not knowing where to go or what to do. Another Zimbabwean student eventually helped me figure out registration and accommodation. It took a long time for me to feel at home.'

I was curious as to his impressions of the city of Nicosia when he first arrived.

'I thought I had come to Europe and expected cold weather with snow and all that but it was the complete opposite,' he laughs. 'It is extremely hot. Also, the buildings in Nicosia looked small and older than I expected. All along I thought I was going to see skyscrapers just like the ones in London or New York. It's not the Europe I had imagined.'

It is still very hard for young Africans to move around the world because of the costs, visa restrictions and terrorism. I wondered if there was a big African presence in Cyprus.

'There is a growing population of Africans, especially students,' he said. 'We are over 20,000 probably, with Nigeria topping, closely followed by Zimbabwe.'

Since he lived in the North, I asked him if he ventured to the south.

'I have never been to the South. By law, we are not allowed to cross over. I am told I need a visa to get there. But what I do know about the South is that it's in the European Union. Goods are cheap there. And all those big multinational companies like KFC, McDonalds and Timberland are found there. We don't have all that in the North.'

'Can you describe Nicosia? What do you like and dislike about the city, the Cypriot mentality and way of life?' I asked.

'Nicosia is very small, at least northern Nicosia. I like the historic walled city and the Kyrenia Gate. I am also fascinated that it is the only divided capital city in the world. I like how they prepare for their national events, decorating the streets and all that.

'In Nicosia, the crime rate is very, very low. No pick-pocketing or even break-ins. I can leave my door unlocked, come back and still find everything intact. The downside, however, is that some shop owners, especially electronic shops, hike their prices because they think African students have a lot of money. House owners too raise rentals frequently. In most cases they require six-month-to-one-year rentals in advance with two months' deposit, which is a big ask.

'They think every African is Nigerian and that every African is either very poor or very rich. There is no in-between. There is also a belief that Africans don't get tired. When you work for them they think that you are a machine and you can do anything they ask you to do. As a people, I find Turkish-Cypriots to be serious. They are not very outgoing but keep a small circle of friends and relatives. This is something I admire about them. They always have time with their families at every gathering, for instance, during the Kurban Bayram holiday, they stay at home with their kids and family, eat and celebrate together.'

The leap from Harare to Nicosia must have been very big. Those of us who leave our homes and cities and find ourselves in other cities of the world, where we begin new lives, inevitably compare them. I asked how the two cities compare and contrast. 'Are there things in Nicosia that remind you of home, the place you left or the place you always imagine home to be?'

'There is nothing much to compare even though they are both developing cities, which are central business hubs to their respective countries. African churches are starting to establish in Nicosia. I go to Forward in Faith Ministries, also known as ZAOGA in Zimbabwe. We fellowship just as we do in Zimbabwe.

'In Nicosia, roads are too narrow and they are all single-carriage. Harare is big, roads are much wider. Harare has taller buildings. Harare has high traffic of people and vehicles, which is not the case in Nicosia.

'The most obvious difference is that public transport here stops operating at 6:00pm in winter and during summer at 7:30pm, unlike in Harare where public transport operates all the time, and with no schedules.

'The Sunday market in Nicosia is the closest experience that reminds me of home. People gather every Sunday at the bus terminal selling wares, fresh fruits and veggies, shouting at the top of their voices, which reminds me so much of Copacabana or Mbare Musika.'

It is hard to live and study far away from home, in a place where you are completely on your own. I ask, 'How do you connect with Zimbabwe – family and friends?'

'New technology – Skype, Imo, WhatsApp and sometimes I buy international phone cards.'

When I left Zimbabwe for the first time I thought moving to a new place would provide all the answers. But I was quick to realise that who you are is always determined by where you are. The bigotries of a foreign place weigh on you sometimes. I have met condescension in the eyes of bank clerks and shop attendants, and malign intent in store detectives trailing me along as I follow the maze of shelves to pick my groceries. 'No? Fact?' I ask.

'I can't say much on that. I think it all depends with the people you meet or interact with. People are different. Some of them really don't tolerate us and see us as nothing. Some believe in brotherhood and say we are the same despite our skin colour, religion or culture.'

Obviously, the education system in Zimbabwe is in a shambles. What is the standard of university education in Cyprus, I want to know. What is it that makes so many young Africans come here?

'Tertiary education is an integral part of government policies here. The whole education system is affiliated with the Higher Council of Education in Turkey, and students receive a quality international standard of education.'

When I lived in a small market town in the south-west of Wales, the only black face I used to see every-day when I woke up was my own. I was the odd one out everywhere I went. The place made me feel different. There is always baggage that comes with that, this feeling that you're constantly on display, being judged and stereotyped and never knowing quite how people feel about you. Sometimes I just wanted to bolt and disappear. 'Do you feel like this sometimes?' I ask.

'I have two memorable experiences. The first was in our school bus coming from school. I once sat next to a Turkish girl, but the moment I sat down she stood up, frowned, crumpled her face, left the seat empty, and stood for the rest of the journey. The second incident was in a supermarket. The till operator refused to serve me. She didn't want to touch my stuff and went on to serve others who were in line behind me until I was the only one left and she told me she was closed. It really got to me and I just walked way. I had nowhere to place a complaint, and, even if I were to do so, they wouldn't listen to me anyway.'

'You have lived in Nicosia for a few years now. What has been your overall experience?'

His response was immediate. 'Overall, my experience has been awesome. I have learnt a new language, Turkish, and have also been exposed to diverse cultures from different parts of the world. I can now also prepare some Turkish dishes,' he laughs. 'Though at times I do miss home, the friendships I have made here also make me feel at home.'

I wondered if there were any other experiences from Cyprus he wanted to share. 'Yeah,' he said. 'Cyprus is expensive, especially for us students who aren't working full-time, because every dollar you receive from home you spend on basic living expenses. It is difficult to secure a job if you don't speak or understand Turkish. There is not much nightlife in Cyprus; if it weren't for the students planning and hosting parties the night life would be just dead.'

SERENDIPITY

Caroline Rooney

It's a long way from Rhodesia to Nicosia,
Past the lowering of the British starburst, ruby
Milk and royal blue, in Africa Unity Square.

Yet outside Ledra Palace jacarandas bloom
The same flurry of mauve on an abrogating sky
As down Rhodes or Herbert Chitepo Avenue.

And the cicada song stays the cicada song,
Sonic sunshine of the present. Indescribable
How nostalgic that track makes me. Cypriots too?

Cicada: the internet says it's from the Latin.
Jacaranda: those globe-trotters South American.
Flora and fauna diaspora, here cohering

OUTER SANCTUM

Caroline Rooney

For Bahriye

Where this begins, recalling that World Poetry Day we celebrated in, or not in, Nicosia, given the dry moat dubbed buffer zone, where the H4C appears maritimely, a ship with a deck, beached yet sailing, buffering the breeze-white flag of art, *amāra* by which we stand, by which we float.

Home for Co-operation, that clear name, suggests we foresee, picturing a balcony above a street that teems with questions, worries, expectations, all human. A hiatus in history dreams of the rain and a river's return. The poems alternate: shelter, harbour, shrine, tent, window open to the weather.

SPATIAL TRIPLING-TRIAD

THE EPIC BOOK OF BAHR BY
THE RED-HAIRED WOMAN OF THE SEA

Bahriye Kemal

Disconnect
Shopping, Un-Documented Nameless, Witch's Cauldron
Three decades, three place names, three
spatial tripling
I cannot navigate
It's not my capital
I prefer it by the sea you see

Sea see
this lack of fit
To sea from the see
tripling capital
captures the truth of
what I sea

Lefkoşa in Three Teen girls,
my good sister, pretty woman, disobedient cousin,
walking down the street
from the former imperial centre London
who searches for three other teen boys
from postcolonial partitioned bandabulya.
What is Nicosia and Λευκωσία?

***

Λευκωσία and Lefkoşa truths in my twenties-3,6,9:

Truth 1. 2002: Not permitted to meet – barriers, borders, censor-
   ship

Waves that shout from my hill to your roundabout

Grivas points to where I long to go

Future global leaders break border law

From Lefkoşa hill we meet in my mother's Pile to your Larnaca

Clandestine crossing (times 3 adding Yazbek's from here I see your
   Jabal Aqraa)

Truth 2. 2003: three oral testimonies on the opening and crossing
   borders

Testimony 1: From Lefkoşa to Istinjon, Κιός, Tabanlı in Paphos,
   Πάφος, Baf

Future global leaders with mother excited (image of experience)

took her to her home

headless chicken,

my grandmother cut it,

your garden (memory shift memory to my childhood)

rummaging ruins

Testimony 2: Doctors from Λευκωσία to Grandma in *Geçitkale*

Am I a settler, an occupier?

Testimony 3: Dad from Nicosia to Κοφίνου, *Köfünye*

Doors closed doors, a Cypriot door, now padlocked

Keys

my dad the *kuyucu*

Keys

my dad the *kuyucu*

Keys

My dad the *well digger*

Truth 3. 2004:
Documents without Names/Nameless offspring of
back and forth
to give and receive documents
a stateless offspring of an avenue along the river,
Shakespeare avenue, Makarios street
when he was told he is a stranger to his name
offspring of whips cross on Mehmet Akif Avenue
when I was told nine months ago you had to change my name.

Three Witches
Thrown into
Cauldron
I grab the handle
My right leg drenched in the boiling potion
It's not dissolving nor burning – no feeling
It's bubbling
Drop-bits thrown up
In my crutch
I will not dissolve into this potion
Drop-bits thrown out
From my crutch
Red flag, blue flag, white flag
Hellim, tzatziki, zeytin,
Molokhia
Donkey on wild donkey
They killed my father
they are 'true' Cypriots
Magic words of bedtime stories
Linobambakoi
All the names you ever know
They are not dissolving.

Nalbantoğlu Hospital (Cheating Death)
For all the African students in Cyprus
Lefkoşa told me the truth.

No Eyes
No mouth
Face now
Bluish mauve red
Swollen
Eyelids
Busted
Lower lip

'stop him, stop him, he did it', the secretary said
'the black dogs did it,' the Irish woman said

'UP, UP,   GOW   GOW, NAW NAW
hade hade' the police said

'raiDed our halls
Gun forced us   aut aut aut Aut Aut Aut AUt AUt AUT AUT
    OUT
Half naked, half sleep   lined us up   Beat us
                    down   at midnight'
my students said

'we didn't do it' they said

'They beat and raped her ...
The Lebanese student' they all said

All 333 were my students.

Nicosia held the truth
It would tell me.

The white bed sheets buried the left,
busted bottom lip covered mouth
explosively bulging eyelid covered face,
Of her face now blue red

She turned left
Gripped hand
Her eyes couldn't speak
       Were they black?
Her lower lip shrivelled
       Did blacks do this?
Her eyelid tinkled
       Were they three black boys?
They all moved in motion
Left to right
    tfel ot thgiR
Left to right
With sound

'No no no black
Yes three
Not African.'

Λευκωσία told me the truth.

          ***

Lefkoşa, Nicosia, Λευκωσία in my thirties
The cauldron took her in
She drank it

tripping
the red-haired woman of the sea
bahr bahr bahr
deniz بحـر θάλασσα
Sea see sea
The book of the sea
The book of navigation
The book of Bahr
Kitab-ı Bahriye
She saw it from the see you sea
name game, number games, competing maps, complex tales, lost
    in trails
childhood bedtime stories narrated by her grandmothers
read bedtime stories narrated by their grandmothers
she hid in the spaces of forbidden games –
'a wave from the sea, I see it from this balcony,
it rests on the shores of the island of Cyprus
the balcony of the Mediterranean Sea.
    A wave from the see. I sea it from this balcony,
and I, I, I won't be a wave from the sea.
Nicosia is in the margins of his poem
the Kurd and Arab
Barakat and Darwish
Like you, all I have is the wind and the wave from the sea' –
poisoned by truths

Truth: I am a Zionist
physical form of your occupation
Her nan plants her headless chicken in your garden
Her mum and dad re-construct their refugee childhood in your
    land
Get my family out

Leave
Return returning turn
Let them use their keys
throw away your keys
on my wedding night my nan gave me her three keys
from her bridal home

Truth: I am a Palestinian –
They sold my great aunt
the most expensive girl in the village
Fanara to Jaffa-Al-Birwa-Haifa – to Beirut to Amman –
Trees are not the ribs of my childhood

I may be the poet Barakat Al-Darwish:
Living there, Ledra,
I saw shadows of my lemon tree.
His greatgrandfather planted it
It wasn't mine really.
Shadows of his childhood.
Collecting souvenirs beneath a tree.
Neither lemon nor olive nor orange
Just a tree
Buried beneath is his bag of stones
Guide to the green line
Guard to the green line.

Truth:
I am unfit
'You will not write Nicosia, Lefkoşa, Λευκωσία' they say
'She can't write Cyprus' they say
'It's off the map
She doesn't fit

You will change your name' they say
Differential Cyprus: Map Project

Cyprus Spring 2014
WLA Zone and rising
Crossing north-south checkpoints
Captures Mediterranean fractures.

Here I invented something
We invented something
And I give it to you, all of you
Here is my gift.

Its description:
Marco Polo productions
My red and blue crisscrossed Britain in Λευκόνοικο
Her Palestine de-starred Jordan in Nicosia
Mrs Bones bird Zimbabwe in Güzelyurt
My Japan near the gas fields in padlocked Κόφίνου
Nene, diagnosed my illness as paraphilia, a key fetish,
with BPD – Border-line Partition Disorder
and gave me the filling from the stone sandwich without 'last
    words'
Her blue, white, red France in the city of the sea
The cigarette claimers five starred china in Ayios Dometios
And upside-down Russia in Lefkoşa
Her red and white starred Turkey in Ammochostos
Her cedar green Lebanon in Yalova
The dead twin's blue Greece in Gazimağusa
My ordered and progressed Brazil near the water pipeline in
    Kyrenia
The heaven breath daughter's blue and red America in Λευκωσία

My Cuba in Famagusta
Paralysed, look to the sea begging for their words
                              our words
Letters on a promise and self-deception
The Great Trek through buzzing bees and sphinx alertness in a
    chocolate standing mountain
Meeting a fire collector with no name who took the one white
    hair on my head
Suffocated by cellophane
These ripe words danced with identity
Our colourful worlds and words poured into Cyprus and the sea.

Now, take the gift and nail it like LAC
Here is a pen
Flag up you mum's village, your dad's village, your nan's village,
    and your sea
Big up your places and your differential spaces
Open it, connect it, detach it, reverse it, tear it, modify it, work it,
Make it your shifting ground between deconstruction and recon-
    struction
Mapmaking and mapbreaking
                    You can do this can't you?
                    Amused at this rhizomatic play.
He has invented something
They have invented something
And they give it to you, all of you
Here is the gift:

Its description
Two pieces of rectangular fabric, both 100% InvistaSolarMax
    nylon
Aspect Ratio: 2:3

One red and white, the other copper and green

Now take one of these gifts, and cherish it
Colour your road, your door, your house, your bed with it
Cry for it, kill for it, die for it
Edify your people to shed their blood for it
Warm your child's cold corpse with it
                    You won't will you?
                    Appalled at this irrationality

So why is it that the tenants of this world
Cry, kill and die for it
Edified, now their burnt bodies are coloured in the grave with it?

Even the worldy tenants
I set out to play and disrupt it
But it played with us, it manipulated and disrupted us
It disturbed and tortured me.
It came alive you know, it spoke to us
About recognition, legal states, illegal states, legitimisation, ille-
    gitimisation
Inclusions, exclusions, rights and no rights
They came alive you know, and they abused and beat me.

Panic sprint, ears waxed, eyes taxed
Failed attempts to secrete with night blooming brides
We emptied the map of red and white, of copper and green
Drained out the blood and moon, swept out the olives and stars,
    wiped out the island
Emptied Cyprus of these nylon flags.

With my friend's dead twin, I gathered the nylon

Two separate standing bundles, beside Victoria secret samples
This for thongs and C-strings, that for push bras and tassels
The residual nylon for couture angel keyhole teddies

Trrrrum-t
    Trrrrum-t
        Trrrrum-t
  trak tiki tak trak tiki tak
Trrrrum-t
    Trrrrum-t
        Trrrrum-t
  trak tiki tak trak tiki tak
Worn at the exhibition
I give them to you, all of you, here is the gift

A well digger found Zeus's gold head
In Turkey
Carried there from Athens
They asked my dad to help them
Sell it, sell it, sell it
To the British museum
I said 'no'

'officials in the north, in the south, in the centre
In Nicosia, Λευκωσία, Lefkoşa
In former imperial centre London
In ethnic mother centre Athens
In ethnic mother centre Ankara
In the east, in the west, in the centre
soon you will be tripping on the 'differential space' potion from
    the witch's cauldron made by me'
says the red-haired woman of the sea

SMALL STORIES OF LONG DURATION

CONJECTURES AROUND A
VANISHED NICOSIAN BATH SIGN

Sevina Floridou

Fig.1. Vanished sign over bath-house entry reading (top) Greek, 'Greek Bath', (centre) English, (bottom) the owner's partially blacked out name, A ... N. Kollitiri

A modern sign reading 'ΕΛΛΗΝΙΚΟΝ ΛΟΥΤΡΟΝ' (Greek bath), with 'TURKISH BATH' in English underneath, used to hang over the south entry of the Ottoman bathhouse, opposite Omeryie mosque in Nicosia. These baths were built when conquering admiral Lala Mustapha Pasha converted the twelfth-century cathedral of St Mary of the Augustinians into a mosque in 1570–79 CE. He also endowed the Omeryie complex with an aqueduct and new bathhouse. The twentieth-century sign disregarded the name by which the building is colloquially known, following mid-twentieth-century politics, by writing it in 'pure' (katharevousa) Greek as masculine, i.e. 'Loutron'. Meanwhile spoken Cypriot-Greek genderbends the spoken name to a plural/ feminine, 'Loutra tis Emerkés'. The baths were upgraded in 2003, but despite this, they struggle to remain open today.

With its round domes naturally lit through blown-glass bells, the baths are easily identifiable near the 'OXI' roundabout, a 1944 vehicular breach cutting through the Venetian walls. Today the bath's main south entry, which used to be crowned by the bilingual inscription, faces a parking area (a space that is itself layered with contested names and submerged histories). The building screens Soutsou street, of red-light fame, located behind. A secondary north-facing back door, conveniently but unconventionally led from the domed cool chamber of the baths into Soutsou street, as we shall see below.

Around the time that the building was restored the dilapidated sign vanished, surviving only in my 1987 photograph. All that remained was a white corrugated metal sheet with the bath's and proprietor's names. Originally, the sign would have been flanked on either end with matching trademark medallions of round, red, enamelled Coca-Cola logos, a novelty in 1955 which graced many shops with modern aspirations.

The year 1955 coincides with a time when a national dichotomy appeared, then picked up momentum that oozed through Nicosia's streets, spilling across the whole walled town and halving it into two. At around the same time, the sign manifests the decision of Mr Kollityri (whom we imagine was G/Cypriot) to upgrade his establishment by advertising the most modern of imported soft drinks, thus taking the opportunity to gentrify his establishment. It is not known whether the medallions bore the Greek word Πιες or its counterpart the Turkish İçiniz, enticing/commanding one to 'drink', as seen in similar pictures from the time, in one language or the other, but never both together.

While Greek and Turkish Cypriot sides, through the United Nations Development Programme and European Union mediating agents, are admirably preserving scores of endangered monuments that would otherwise have crumbled, they have agreed to agree, through reconciliatory restoration, to avoid sensitive issues, working with optimum historic phases and removing later interventions. However, to take the baths as an example, is agreeing to wipe out the twentieth century when restoring a building for use in the twenty-first, by regressing to the sixteenth century really the best approach? Especially if a building hosts fragile twentieth-century fragmented stories that have survived the conflict, only to vanish during restoration work.

Soon after 1955, within the enclosed Venetian walls, Nicosia's residents were forced to abandon their homes in waves on finding that their properties and livelihoods were on a 'wrong' side of the flaring conflict. Traders cooperating between communities faced forcible intimidation by nationalist groups from both sides. One early coercion prevented the exchange of money between ethnic 'others'. For example, rentiers were forced to abstain from settling rent between a G/Cypriot renting a house from a T/Cypriot or vice versa. The majority of the formerly rural dwelling population, for whom experiencing such transition to city-life was hard enough, had to suddenly contend with intimidation that struck at the core of their self-esteem, their reputation in society. Honouring timely settlement of one's financial obligations thus escalated very quickly into unspoken treason, subverting paying or receiving rent, into a politicised statement of defiance. An action which was punishable by sniper death.

Coercing people to abandon mixed neighbourhoods by snip-pering those who did not comply must have affected the legibility of the urban cityscape, confusing notions of where it was 'safe' in relation to where 'home' was, as residents hastily relocated, some-times overnight. People were forced to figure out different ways of going about their daily lives in a volatile topography. Public places of interaction, including food markets, cinemas, coffee shops and bathhouses, also became swiftly segregated.

The final split came on the night of 23 December 1963, when a sniper shot Jemalie, an alleged young T/Cypriot prostitute, walking together with her alleged G/Cypriot pimp on the easternmost end of Ermou Street. Riots escalated with the arrival of G/Cypriot police when T/Cypriots were instructed to refuse G/Cypriot authority. Jemalie crawled on for two hundred meters, bleeding to her death as fighting erupted in the streets around her, while the good people of Nicosia would have observed the scene behind their latticed windows. An ambulance arrived for her too late, only after her ordeal by exsanguination was completed, the following morning.

Following the riots, the former colonial authorities, reinstated as peace-keepers, temporarily sealed all side-streets leading onto Ermou with barbed wire. They mapped this hurried line with green pencil onto the city map, naming the agency that still prevents people from the north of the city going to the south and vice versa. The Green Line, enclosing space behind barbed wire, coalesced into a disputed zone. Bordered by not one but two undulating demarcations, north and south, these have together strangled life out of the sprawling market street, its hostels, houses, schools, shops, khans, workshops, churches and mosques. The city's vibrant awakening into modernity, witnessed through twentieth-century modernist architecture beside Ottoman and Venetian structures, has since transformed into a forgotten, hollow city core of undulating width, patrolled by mostly English-speaking UN soldiers.

It is curious therefore to examine how mid-twentieth-century Nicosia's five medieval public baths fared, by coincidence or intent, outside the lines of demarcation, particularly since the first conflict decade (1955–1964) marked a time when there was no other way for most people in the city to bathe.

After the 1964 split, three Ottoman baths inside the walled city, Buyuk, Emir and Korkut Baths, continued catering only to T/Cypriot, north-enclaved residents. Adjacent to the former Armenian neighbourhood, the latter is mapped as a 'women's bath', but it is today in disrepair and recommended online for gay clientele. Emir Hamam is also all but ruined, while Buyuk Hamam (the 'Big' baths), dating to the sixteenth-century and incorporating early fourteenth-century remains, boasts elevated status, renovated by the same bi-communal initiative and funding that has also restored Omeryie Hamam, to the south of the divide. It appears, then, that class and official historic interpretation privilege Nicosia's 'grand' monuments over its subjectified, small-scale 'lay' heritage.

The Tandi Hamam baths, built around 1920 and still landmarking the north-east walled neighbourhood, fell into ruin after 1958, following a retaliation killing of the G/Cypriot owner by T/Cypriot hit men after he disregarded an imposed curfew and crossed to visit his properties that had suddenly found themselves on contested ground to settle payments owed to him. His perfunctory actions led him into a no man's land that may not have yet fully received visual demarcation. Bearing in mind the centuries-old tradition of class rather than ethnic alignment, he would not have heeded killings that had occurred in outlying villages. There might even have been initial disbelief towards a separation contesting religious ethnicity but practically affecting land and property, because the totalitarian grip of factional fighting never gave citizens a chance to voice their opinions or discuss any political terms.

During the 1930s and until its demise, Tandi Hamam was also notorious on account of its proprietress, Simsar Pembe. While conducting traditional women social bathing rituals (pre-nuptial bridal exfoliating, *lehusa* 'after birth' baths, hen nights, male circumcision baths), she was said to have arranged sales of destitute T/Cypriot young women between their guardians and buyers from Palestine or Jordan. She is remembered for preparing the bartered brides' ritual baths in published oral accounts by expatriated matrons. Other accounts, from men, recall how, for a fee, Pembe would allow them to watch the women bathe, presumably unbeknown to the victims.

Although privately piped water gradually became more readily available, this would not account for Tandi Hamam's abandonment, since the fifth bath of Nicosia, Omeryie Hamam, appears to have survived the city's infrastructure upgrade to domestic piped water and private baths. It continued its uninterrupted use without closing once, from its founding around 1579 through the 1964 conflicts, to shortly before its restoration in 2003.

Omeryie Hamam provided its hygienic services indiscriminately to all ethnic and social groups and to all genders, being the only bath south of the divide, in one of the last mixed neighbourhoods. It continued even when all the T/Cypriot residents from adjacent Galip street were moved north during the 1970s, after which it carved a different market niche for itself.

Omeryie Hamam's clientéle would have come from different social classes, as bathing segregation was managed between levels of 'respectability'. Throughout history, neither class nor ethnicity caused problems in Ottoman hamams, which were regulated by strict hierarchies. Each bath was run by a proprietor, sworn by law to uphold a series of 'do's and don'ts'. Rules not only enforced bathing for different classes (e.g. separate days for the girls from the brothels and separate for married women with children), but also religious groups bathed separately, particularly after a law of 1744. Further regulation designated that men and women would bathe separately, on different days and hours of the week, while on specific days the baths could be hired privately by couples.

Let us return to the sign and what it might tell us about the bath's resilience during the twentieth century.

Since religious segregation had been normalised for over two hundred years, why would Kollityri suddenly wish to emphasise a segregated establishment? Was he taking sides in the ethnic division of the city? Why subtitle with 'Turkish Bath' in the face of dwindling T/Cypriots on this side of the city, who were already being purged northwards? Why not claim to be solely a G/Cypriot bath, and comply with his side's nationalist wishes? Was it perhaps in deference to the mosque across the street? Why, in what was otherwise such an unforgiving conflict, would nationalist G/Cypriots put up with a 'Turkish' bath on 'their' south side of town?

Paradoxically, the use of two languages and referencing the two 'bathing-contested ethnicities' might indicate that the sign, and therefore baths, refrained from taking political sides. Using only one language could have resulted in a loss of customers, or even an alienation of friends. Moreover, dividing customers by 'sides' would have been complicated in a town where those 'sides' were being readjusted daily.

Were there people who would not recognise 'Hamam' but would be familiar with 'Turkish bathing', searching for commercial modernity and beguiled by the offer of a cold Coca-Cola? Perhaps it was the Ottoman reference that was being purged by this modern sign, on the face of an otherwise unchanged Ottoman bathhouse. Perhaps T/Cypriots would have welcomed the promise of modernity offered through the English wording, directed at Neo-Turk sensitivities.

A triple manipulation emerges. The three masculine groups to whom the male-gendered sign is addressed would never actually have to cross paths on the premises. T/Cypriot nationalists would have been appeased, since their presence was validated; the 'Greek Bath' signifier kept nationalist G/Cypriots satisfied. Appeasing both nationalist fantasies allowed the baths to remain operating. Kollitiri in fact may have cleverly devised how to use the new sign as an apotropaic banner, proclaiming English 'protection' whilst upgrading the establishment with a casual Coca-Cola advertisement. Meanwhile, all three groups continued rampaging against one another on the streets outside.

This sign shows that, during the conflict decades, the British may not always have been perceived as enemies by G/Cypriot nationalists, subverting today's rhetoric of an absolute anti-colonial sentiment – the proof being that, with its English script, the sign remained in place for over forty years. The 'Turkish Bath' neologism probably targeted English soldiers-turned-peace-keepers patrolling the streets. Seeking refuge under their patronage, Kollityri may have established the only neutral zone within the city, visited by all conflicting sides, through their shared need for cleanliness. For, although strictly forbidden to visit brothels on Soutsou street, the British soldiers could bathe. The soldiers' secret hunt for a brothel could be a possible reason for the bath's back door, which opened directly into the red-light district.

For me, the vanished sign, together with the back door that was sealed during restorations for not complying to an Ottoman optimum phase, offered conjectures on an Aristophanian level (recalling Dikaiopolis, the Acharnean protagonist, who miraculously obtains a private peace treaty with both the Spartans and their enemies the Athenians). Yet the sign's cheek simultaneously also evokes the stoic qualities of Karagöz, Καραγκιόζης (for G/Cypriots), a subversive character from folk shadow-theatre beloved by both communities. One can imagine Kollityri as a surly Monty Python-esque black-comedy anti-hero, fusing a character across genres and centuries, celebrated by surviving on his wits, doing business while minding his own. An enterprising make-do and mend individual, inviting all the actors inside, in a precarious Nicosia, balancing emergent conditions of drama and conflict in the city. Meanwhile, beneath the dome of steam, tranquillity would suffuse more personal woes, as it always had.

Apart from the bath proprietor, keenly alert to whatever might shatter the fragile peace of his livelihood (social causes, as well as the workings of ageing brass boilers, clay pipes and stone water tanks), a daily choreography can be imagined, stretching into time-cycles, involving a variety of social actors passing through the steam infused space. Possibly a naive sidekick for odd jobs, a shrewd Mrs. Kollityri dispensing advice and managing the scrubbers attending to the bathers: the *tellaks* and *natirs*. *Natirs* were aged, destitute prostitutes, the most downtrodden social class, but with a special role in society before weddings. In addition to preparing the bride in her pre-nuptial ceremony, *natirs* explained the facts of life to brides-to-be before their wedding night, since it was socially unheard-of for respectable mamas to conduct this sort of talk with their daughters.

Distortions of reality occurred inside the steam-bath. Green henna mud, smeared on hair above white kaolin face masks, looming through roof-lit steam over curvaceous soap-lathered bodies, must have presented Fellini-esque imagery. On completing their cleansing rituals, families would leave through the front door followed by their child-servants (another unaddressed under-privileged class), carrying the family's bundle of soaps, toiletries, *peshkir* flannels, clothes, *nalums*, and left-over finger-foods such as *dolma* and *baklava*, for bathing would take hours to complete properly. In through the back door would come the schoolboys, after their deflowering initiation in Soutsou street. On other nights, the *esnaf* (joint guilds) would book the hamam to hold their own long-forgotten rituals, which would raise apprentices to the level of masters.

While Nicosia slowly succumbs to the continuing half-century conflict, perishable moveable cultural artefacts alluding to a bicommunal past are continuously vanishing. For many of today's inhabitants of this part of town – temporarilry underprivileged migrants of various ethnicities – the entry fee to the restored, new-age establishment is too expensive to render particular significance, either to them or to the town's need for varied social space. That the neighbourhood would perhaps benefit from modern public bathing facilities is something to contemplate, since few spaces within the walled town have ever addressed class-defying social interaction, and, from a practical perspective, few of today's leased properties in the area have adequately upgraded their plumbing since the conflicts.

Today's 'historically' restored baths, sanitised to twenty-first-century standards, offering Chinese health-spas, bachelors' and hens' nights to hip Nicosians, dare them to experience or re-invent an eclectic orientalist fantasy. One too close to home, perhaps, or irritatingly, for some, the wrong fantasy altogether. Set in a poor neighbourhood that they are disconnected from, the new spa-baths sit uncomfortably with their restored version of an imagined community.

There is every need to look at the 'breakage' both in the time-line and the materiality of historic conflict-zone buildings, and see restoration not merely as a technical problem but as a challenging layer of social history. Recognising the messy periods, such as the ravages of lengthy neglect through a bottom-up, grassroots history, is important. Such periods are testament to social resilience. Proof that these baths functioned for a long time before their fixing means that small stories of long duration can sometimes be equal in importance to whatever monumental top-down restoration is hoping to address.

We will never know how the artful Kollytiri managed daily

events, balancing actors for as long as he did. We can only guess through his name, or nickname, which alludes to the hapless sidekick son of Karagiözis. In the shadow theatre, the character of Kollitytri unwittingly (or not) always bungles his father's schemes (like Comedia del'Arte's servant sidekick), exposing the fallacies of the upper classes and rulers, to the audience's delight. And, like the best of puppet-masters, Mr Kollytiri, the bath proprietor of Omeryie Hamam, will remain in the shadows of conjecture, behind the sign that vanished.

RHAPSODY ON THE DRAGOMAN

Stephanos Stephanides

For Susan and Harish, νψίστους διδασκάλους

Part I
I am a dragoman
courtesan of the word
I pluck my eyes to hear
with skill and improvisation
wor-l-ds of hard edges,
a treacherous and loyal
exponent of obsessions
not all men know my speech

in the night I go under
in company of dervishes and learn
why cyclamens sprout in pavement cracks
and mutter promises, amidst the dust,
of the beautiful and the unseen
I ask meaning for
Fore give fore go fore play
an island warbler
still with no quarrel
or a swallow
in the line of flight
meandering with finality
knowing that the road is lost

in floating debris
of fortuitous choices
precipitous moves

with impulsive sagacity
I swirl and sail away
vexed in my state of grace
daytime dragoman
nighttime dervish

Part II
When hearts hum in the buzz
of morning light so bright it silences,
the lady arrived at the City Gate
and waited for the *tarjuman*
she had requested in a letter sent from Egypt,
someone versed in her language
to accompany her to the Sublime Porte.
Only I among the *rayahs* spoke her tongue
from that island in the northern sea.
Today, following my companion's counsel
 I shed my *kufta* and *jubbeh*,
and present myself with *boyunbagi* and waistcoat in a style
after the French.

I bow and before she presumes
to scrutinise the measure of my wisdom
If I am a fool servant or a learned scholar
I do not climb inside the carriage
I swiftly step up to the box instead and take my seat
next to the driver while I instruct the porter boy
if he receives *bakshish* to say 'thank you' as her kind expect,

and reveal neither gratitude nor displeasure;
she need not know our measure of her generosity,
only count the day's profit within our own walls;
we do not know
if she desires the sweetness of the sultanina grape
or some other island sweetness.
When heaven wants to speak
 it needs few words
to open gateways here, there, and elsewhere.
Trees grow in silence
as do the date-palms lining the river
inside the city wall.

Along the path of Hermes
the wind will track the language down
as we track the dust of love
in the mausoleum smell of mourning
jasmine turning putrid.
When the evening drops stealthily
I will retire to the Dragoman's house
where hot stone will transform my body to vapory waters
absorbing the contours of the cypress
with long shadows of night in a crimson trance
penetrating the skylight of the hamam
yearning neither joy nor melancholy.
Time to appease my travelling consciousness.
On the divan I will translate for my companions
Verses of the *Tarjuman al-ashwaq* of Ibn Arabi
My heart takes on any form.

RIGHT HAND CORNER

Christodoulos Moisa

Gogo wake up! Get dressed and get your arse around here.
    Where?
    Spiros's. I got a room. The one they play poker in.
    Why the hurry?
    I have a deal. And be quick about it. I haven't got all day. It's big
and there's money to be made.
    Money?
    Ten million.
    Euros or dollars?
    Pounds.
    I'm coming. Thirty minutes!

***

Why did you ring him?
    He's a fuckin' engineer, Taki. He'll tell us if it can be done?
    It can be done.
    Not if we take the whole wall down.
    The three sides and the skeleton can hold it up.
    What, you are an engineer now?
    No, but they used to build them to last.
    Yeah, but the lopsided weight might topple it over.
    It should be fine.
    Well, Gogo will tell us.
    And what about the owner?

He is creaming himself. Since the haircut, the place had been empty. The stupid shit charged the place off the market, and now that all the shops have moved to Ledra he is losing money hand -over-fist.

How much are you giving him?

Five hundred thousand.

And he keeps the place ...

That's what she said.

She doesn't want to buy it?

No. It's all here in the contract. She wants a window to be built that takes up the whole facade.

Is that all?

No. She says it's got to be a golden rectangle.

What's a golden rectangle?

It's a special rectangle from the ancient Greeks.

And ...?

It's also got to be black glass.

Fuck, that is going to be hard. That's a huge piece of glass.

She doesn't mind if it's in panels.

Why is she doing this?

Fucked if I know.

Have you met her?

When we signed the deal.

What's she like?

She waltzed in wearing a singlet, shorts and flip-flops. She's not very tall. Eyes as black as coal. Swears like one of those Greek officers we used to have. She speaks Greek too, like one of us, but she looks Turkish.

You look Turkish.

No I don't.

Then like an Arab.

No I don't.

What about you?

I look like a Greek.

What, because you got blue eyes?

Well, there's that.

Anyway what's a Greek?

Blue-eyed blonds.

How many blue-eyed blonds you know?

A –

Yeah, well she also spoke perfect English.

I speak English.

Greeklish.

It gets me by.

Yeah right.

Where has she made her money?

Well the down payment cheque is from a London bank so probably there. But she could have made it anywhere.

You don't think she's a drug trafficker or something?

I thought of that. More like a brothel owner.

You mean she's into sex trafficking?

Could be. Or she could be a gun runner or something.

Maybe we should give it a miss?

Are you crazy? It's probably one of those start-up things. Those computer geeks make millions and don't know where to spend it.

I still say let's give it a miss.

Don't be stupid. Something like this comes around once in a lifetime. It's lucky that I was in the office when she came. Otherwise, someone else would have hijacked her.

What if the Minister hears about it?

I'll give him a cut.

How many know about it?

You and me ... and Gogo will have to know. You heard all he knows. I'll tell him when he comes over.

So you are saying nothing more to the owner?

Why should I? He's quite happy with his cut.

What did you tell him?

I spun him some bullshit story.

What's that?

That there's a sculptor who is doing a Christo-like thing and wants to install a large window on his building.

Who is Christo?

He and his wife were artists. They used to wrap things up like a package. Big things, like the Parthenon, the Pont-Neufand in Paris and things.

Why did they do that?

Fucked if I know.

The owner bought it?

Well, not at first. You know how we are. He smelled money and was suspicious. I had to show him some photos of the Christo things on my phone. He seemed satisfied but I wouldn't be surprised if he plants someone when we are building to find out more. So don't get pissed and start shouting it from the roofs-tops, eh?

Who, me?

Yes, you. Remember that thing with the traffic cameras. Don't look at me like that. You know what I am talking about. I had the Minister all sewed up and he finally got the whole cabinet behind him. That privacy idea worked. Even after the cameras were installed the House still put an end to it. They were terrified that the cameras would snap them with their girlfriends sitting next to them if they were speeding. Even the queers voted for it. Then the shit hit the fan after you told that bitch of yours. You know ... that reporter you were trying to impress so you could get into her pants. Luckily the cameras were up and the deal was finished by then. So this is top secret. That's if you value your cut.

Trust me. I'm not stupid.

Well, I don't want some other bastard taking this over.

Can you handle it with everything else you got on?

It'll be hard, but I can juggle things around. I can fit it in, no problem. Instead of going to Rosa's in the afternoon after work I'll go to my parents' flat in Onasagorou. You'll find me there after work. I'll set it all up. It will be my headquarters for the project. You'll be my eyes and ears on the ground.

Where are they now?

Who?

Your parents.

At an old people's home. My father has gone gaga.

Poor sod.

No more than he deserved. He ate and drank himself into a barrel and fucked every whore in Soutsou Street.

What, your old man?

Yeah. You'll never think it eh. Ugly has nothing to do with it if you have money.

Yeah. So you are a chip off the old block?

What are you talking about?

It's a saying.

I don't whore around. Rosa is a good girl. She works hard at that TV station. But I have my needs. If my wife gave me one even once in a while, I wouldn't have strayed. But she's found God. He must give her something that I can't.

Maybe she's having it off with the priest?

Are you fuckin' crazy?

What?

What? Don't you dare talk about my wife like that!

Sorry Bambo. I am just joking.

Well, don't joke when it concerns my wife. She's given me three kids. I am doing this for them.

We are all doing it for our kids.

Yes we are. And don't you forget it. Not even to your wife or that Philippineza you are fuckin'.

I won't.

Here's Gogo. Yiassou Gogo!

Hi lads. You know Stavros.

What? Why the fuck is he here?

He is my son.

So?

He's a good lad.

I asked you why he is here?

He's unemployed.

So?

Well, he'll work with us on the project.

As what?

I'll work at anything Kyrie Charalambe.

I am not talking to you numbskull. I am talking to your father.

Come on Bambo. The lad needs work. You know how it is since the haircut. It's either he sits all day on a cup of coffee at a kafenio or work in a café for three euros an hour.

The café is work.

No, we have the blacks for that.

What blacks?

You know, the Indians and the Asians.

For what?

They do those jobs.

There are no jobs.

Those foreigners take our kids' work.

So your son is prepared to change my father's nappies?

Of course not. He has a degree from London.

Yeah. He took eight years to finish a four-year degree. Anyway the cheapest thing in this little paradise of ours is a degree, Gogo. Go home Stavros and if I think of anything I'll call you.

Okay, Kyrie Charalambe. Yiassas.

Pigene sto kalo.

Yiassou my son. I'll see you tonight.

Okay father. Yiassas.

Close the door as you go out Stavro.

Okay.

Are you fuckin' stupid or something Gogo?

What?

What? Bringing your little princeling with you.

I told you the boy needs a job.

Okay. Maybe down the track I'll find him something. I am trying to run a tight ship here. So don't go telling anything to anyone about this. There's a million in it for you if you play your part.

What's the project?

We got to hang a large window on the side of that ugly thing outside the city walls. You know Polemis's Victoria thing.

What sort of window?

A black thing. No light has to come out of it in the night if someone switches on, even a bulb. Also it's got to cover all ten storeys.

Oh, is that all?

No! It's got to be a golden rectangle.

What?

It's a Carbushier type of thing.

Who the fuck is that?

Carbushier. The French architect.

Oh you mean Corbusier ... Le Corbusier?

Yeah him.

He was Swiss.

Whatever.

A golden rectangle?

Yeah.

What for?

Fucked if I know. This bitch wants a window hung and she's willing to pay for it.

How much do I get?

I told you. A million.

No! That's not enough. A million two fifty.

You little turd!

Million two fifty.

I could have gone with Markos but I decided to go with you.

Go with Markos then. Million three hundred.

Okay. Okay. Wanker!

What about me Bambo?

What about you?

I should get another three hundred too.

What you should get is a kick up the bum Taki. All you have to do is be there on the job and sell it to the Union. I'll give you some grease money for that. Yes for Gogo. Yes, because we need him. But no for you, no increase.

But –

No buts. If you give me any grief, I'll start wishing that I left you up on the Pentadactylo and let the Turks put you out of your misery in '74. Instead, I carried you all the way to fuckin' Lefkosia and all the way to the hospital ...

Okay! Okay, forget about it.

No, I won't forget about it. Don't try pulling one like that again.

I'm sorry Bambo.

Now listen carefully. Everyone in the Government offices, I'll deal with. Taki I want you to ring your travel agent mate and get us a dozen packages to London and get him to throw some cruises in. They are the latest rage. As I said you deal with the Union. I don't want them squeezing too much out of us. Tell them if they don't play ball we'll get some Albanians or Indians to do the work. I am going to Qatar next week – tell them the Indians or Pakistanis there will pay us to come and work here. I saw the conditions they work in when I was there last with the Minister on that trade deal. Now, Gogo, you get to tell me if it can be done. You are the engineer. Can that old piece of shit hold that weight without toppling over?

Well, it will be hard. There's a steel frame for the weight of the glass ... it will have to be plate glass ... and probably we'll have to reinforce the interior pillars ... old concrete corrodes ...

***

'Mister President, Honourable Ministers, your Beatitude, Ladies and Gentleman. It is with great honour and considerable pride as the project manager that, tonight, on this beautiful summer's night under a full moon, I will be asking his beatitude our Church's Arch-bishop to unveil the rejuvenation of what is one of our city's oldest colonial buildings. Built last century by Athanasios Prokopi, one of our most famous expat entrepreneurs, the strengthening and modernization of this building named after Queen Victoria will ensure that it lasts another one hundred years. Other than the London-based financier many people contributed towards the realisation of this project. Among those are two architects, two engineers and five interior designers. Another much needed international component of this project was specialist trained labour which was attracted from Qatar. That we lost two of those Indian employees during the project is a tragedy, and my sympathy goes to their families. Ladies and Gentlemen, can I please ask everyone to stand for a minute of silence in memory of those two men who sacrificed themselves in the realisation of this project. Thank you, Lefkosia.'

***

EIGHT PEOPLE WERE KILLED AND TENS OF OTHERS injured after the unveiling of the newly restored Victoria building, on Stasinou Avenue outside the walls of the old city of Lefkosia. The incident happened late on Tuesday night of the summer solstice. The President has ordered the Minister of Interior to carry out a full investigation. The individuals who lost their lives in the disaster have not yet been named. A young man who recently graduated from a London University and worked on the project is currently being held on remand.

According to a source close to the investigation, who did not want to be named, it is suspected that the aforementioned graduate allegedly procured faulty cement from Romania for the project. Apparently, the cement's use-by-date had expired and because of this it was available for a third of the price. The young man has been charged with manslaughter and fraud. His father, an eminent Cypriot businessman, said that his son 'is innocent as he was only employed as a warehouse manager.' He has hired the finest legal firm on the island, and he is confident that his son will be found not guilty. A representative for the financier of the project said that 'She's an artist but is not stupid.' The finance of the restoration was insured. According to the spokesman, the financier and self-proclaimed installation artist will be investing the compensation into another project, possibly in northern Cyprus. Her company is called Creative Collateral Damage. Below is a picture of the building after it was unveiled and prior to its collapse. Note the full moon at the top right-hand corner.

I MADE A PROMISE TO BLUE

Jenan Selçuk

Written on the anniversary of his death,
with Kaya Çanca

Translated by Aydın Mehmet Ali

Just as the moon does
night after night I nurture suicide,
    suckling it on verses
Shedding light on its darkness

I burnt! All the cities that poems ran through
along with the poems that ran through the city of Şeher

I did! I gave my word to Blue

You assumed I would acquiesce, as I stared into the flames

I was on fire as I wrote your eyes

You were hesitant. Only once dead
would you be able to give up dying

NICOSIA

Rachael Pettus

The city
is a rounded star bisected,
bastion-barbed;
a throwing star that spins out seasons
into years;
a capital of light
with minarets that pierce the sky;
hidden pocket gardens,
and arches that soar and hold
up time.

Down-time
and the streets are lit and bustling;
fruit and flowers hang, mingling their fragrances
with spices,
and coffee,
and roasting meat.
The heat of summer makes the gutters stink of history.

In January, the streets are paved
with the leather skins
of last year's pomegranates,
yet still the hodja sings
and still the church bells clamour
on the breeze.

IN THE COMPANY OF BIRDS

Angus Reid

What happened up there?

For six weeks I sat and painted from the roof of Selimiye Camii, Ayia Sophia, the great gothic pile that commands the centre of Nicosia. And since then I have been unable to paint and draw, unable to focus my eyes or my thoughts.

What happened up there?

I found myself in Nicosia. I found the person with the nerve to paint in the street. Nicosia taught me that the artist has a place in the street and that the street esteems the artist. Thumbs up from the kids. Those who couldn't understand were tourists. They couldn't understand that the Green Line, its shattered buildings and the people clustered in its shadow, are beautiful. The broken streets of Nicosia fed me, esteemed me, and took me with tolerance. They invited me to dare and to carry on daring. So, what happened up there?

Just because people pick territorial fights, like cats, doesn't mean that they don't share the sky, like birds. The invitation had been there from the start. Nicosia asked, and waited for me for a lifetime. Nicosia forgot, but remembered me when I returned, thirty years later. Nicosia and I picked up where we had left off as though I had never been away. Nicosia wanted to extend the conversation. The kids of Victoria Street had shown me their birds, their evening squadron. There, cradled in a boy's hands, was the being to become, whose home is the sky, whose eye and instinct is immediate.

'Become like us', said the bird. 'Know the light that turns in the sky. Leave the streets. Seek the exuberance of the light and the wind and the rooftops. There is another horizon, beyond the labyrinth of men.' So, after all the work below, padding and sniffing and watching and working in the streets, Nicosia drew me upwards, onto the roofs and into the view of the wholeness of itself. There on my own I was never alone. It was as though the city in its elemental form wrestled with me. The angel must have seen that Jacob was fit to wrestle, at long last.

Of course, we call that path spiritual. In Nicosia that path exists and it goes like this: shoes off; *as-salamu alaykum*; a hidden key; a door unlocked; shoes on; a spiral stair; a long gallery; a spiral stair; many nests and feathers; a second door, this time fragile and transparent; a narrow bridge, and then the immense welcome of that hot roof.

Open in all directions, with only the company of birds. Are you swift, swift enough? Can you bear to spend days and weeks only in the company of birds?

I square up to the line where land and sky are folded, the vanishing point of the Mesaoria. I find a quarter-ton beam of wood to weigh me down, to secure my unfeathered body in this world of wind and euphoria. I store my tools, my canvas and palette where the pigeons go to hide. I begin the translation of my senses into light. The force that buoys and carries the birds will be my element.

And what force.

Its first question is: are you strong? Are you strong enough? If you are not strong enough, I shall destroy you. My canvas, lashed to the beam, my palette taped to my thigh, my left hand rigid to hold the shaking canvas, my body weight plus that quarter-ton offcut, and all these are still not enough as the great hot breath courses in, gleeful to find a plaything, and it lifts me like a windsurfer. It lifts the whole apparatus into the air. It plays me to the limits of my body-weight. I feel it challenge me to surrender, to give up. I bow my head. I wrestle.

For three days I wrestle with the angel, the wind from one quarter. The third day is the most extreme. By sunset I am exhausted. I have fought all afternoon in a wild gritty struggle, knowing that I am at my own limit. I have to improvise all the time to stay in control, to keep my things from being snapped away, and to achieve a sense of what the light is doing to the diagonals of the market roof, to the ghostly forms of the Troodos, to the toothy runtishness, the concrete stumps of skyscrapers. In the rush, the wind-abraded view, it simplifies. Paint it all again. And again. All of it. Move the eye from the form to the sky, and back, and back to the horizon, as each element changes and changes, the hot torrent of angel breath threatening disaster and never letting up, relentlessly testing and rattling and honing me into its playmate.

The thing is done. My skin still bristles with wind-burn. The last touch was two wind-torn swifts, and my canvas is propped in the circular stair-well to dry. With a few feathers stuck to it, along with a spattering of the small sticks and stones that the wind carries on its tongue.

I can't think. I had to stop. The painting was a crescendo of conflict. But that wind, that keening bright eye, is as fierce as ever. I have no idea whether the painting is good or bad, but it exists. The angel was merciful.

***

Ahmet shows me a calligraphy, made in the seventeenth century, that has gone to Istanbul for restoration. A work that was created in the mosque, and that has always been in the mosque. Square, like my canvases. It is an economical compound of my ideas. Each corner contains the name of an angel. These names, in loops and ties, read across the page, each pathway making meanings. Four corners. Four quarters of the compass. Four angels.

Would you recognise an angel?

I explain my drawings to the Imam. Or rather, because the Imam is praying, I explain to the guardian how, from the roof, I can see into the streets and courtyards of the city and look up to connect them to the horizon. Then I watch as my gestures are repeated by the guardian as he explains to the Imam. The first time I saw my sketchbook hurry across the carpet to that distant, Mecca-facing corner, I stood with my heart in my mouth. Then the Imam turned to face me, with a thumbs-up.

***

I drag my beam over the hump-backs of the vault, and set up above the prayer-place, looking south-east, aligning with the counter-axis by which Islam has adjusted the Frankish Gothic to itself. This is a complex image that looks over the sandstone of the buttresses, into the courtyard of the Eaved House and out towards the Archbishop's palace: a maze of streets and palms within the flat circumference of Venetian walls. I am looking deep into the fabric of division.

Dinda sees me at work and snaps me on her iPhone.

I am investigating shapes of which I am ignorant. The work goes slowly and methodically, and the canvas seems vast. This time, unforced by a jet-stream of wind, I work slowly and descend into the neighbourhoods to investigate the streets I am painting. When I am confused, generalisation will not do. There is, for example, a dark area behind the palace that I don't understand, and it is not until we find a vast and gloomy cypress, ringing with birdsong, that those millimetres make sense. The Green Line, so obvious at street level, is more or less imaginary, and of no compositional significance.

I am told to stop.

Ahmet, who has been my enabler and companion over coffee, has been called in the middle of the night by people who demand that I stop. I know that just as I can see, so I am seen by the three military forces. Our friend in the UN – a patient captain – has said with a smile that he deduced the lonely silhouette on the roof to be me. And if he saw me, then so have the listless legions of the Turkish and Greek military. Maybe you are a spy, says Ahmet. Maybe you are planning to make some chaos. He can counter my protest with a shrug: this is Cyprus, man. Try to be finished today.

But I cannot be finished today. The painting has multiplied into hundreds of miniature city portraits sewn together – street, palm, wall, roof – and my task is to find the rhythm through the elements, that metal yard, that Green Line gate, that church ... But now, as I work, I have the sensation that I am watched. I have the sensation of my body in the cross-hairs of a telescopic sight. I imagine, quite suddenly, the impact of a bullet. This is the test of the second angel. The paranoia.

If I persist, I risk losing my life. I also risk losing my friendship with Ahmet and the easy tolerance I have won in the mosque. But I am unsatisfied with the painting. It has to work through the pattern of the lived city, the political fabric. Now that I am not being hurried by the wind I can see what a blessing the wind had been. This is the opposite, slow and pedantic, and I am bogged down in detail.

At some point, on that day, as the sun turns and slides from one pattern of shadows to another, a door opens on a roof opposite and a boy appears. He sees me. He waves cheerfully. A boy from that mortar-flecked block, bang in the centre of my painting. I paint the open door.

Years ago, thirty years ago, when I first painted in Nicosia, no-one had a camera on their phone. No-one even had a phone. A camera had a different status: a camera was a weapon. So I took no photos. I used the antiquated clobber of easel, palette and canvas. Of sugar-paper and charcoal. Of pencil and sketchbook. When questioned, I showed. I grew accustomed to the idea that people should see over my shoulder. I realised that the art must be accurate and figurative, and that I might be able to profit from the discipline. It kept me keen to the reality. As I paint again, nothing has changed. As I look down from the roof, where no one visits me and my body shrinks from the invisible touch of cross-hairs, I think that I shall invite these midnight whisperers, these people that torment Ahmet with anonymous phone-calls, to come and see what I am doing. To see that my easel has no technology of surveillance, no secret aerial, no recording device. It is just what you need for patient observation. I explain – in a monologue to the pigeons – that I am there all day simply to gather the whole day's light into the image, the whole radiance from morning to evening.

The next day I am ready for them, and I persist. This is about the colours within which people live. The hot concrete and the dry shade. Below my feet, in tessellated orange and buckled planes of terracotta, is the defining light. It's a curious universal light, a kind of loving illumination within the whole view. How this will work is unknown to me, but it unfolds as the painting proceeds. As though the canvas were the means, across every centimetre of its surface, to ensure that attention has been distributed evenly. Until it becomes a little ridiculous that the adjacent marks of this neighbourhood, Indian red, and this neighbourhood, white, have never met. Ridiculous that the two colours live side by side in a wilful separation.

And as I run through these thoughts, my body, that has been cringing from the imaginary bullet, relaxes. I am reassured by my own monotone. I have more permanence than this jittery paranoia. I can outlast its assault.

Was that a second angel, that sought to part my soul from my body?

Below my feet, a woman with a headscarf sits and consults her phone. My last touch is to paint her in, tiny, but real.

***

I leave the painting in the gallery at the west end of the nave. Enough wind and feathers and grit. It can harden amongst the murmurings of prayer.

Ahmet is oddly relieved that I didn't give up. I tell him that I'm done with views southwards across the Green Line. I tell him the soldiers won't see me anymore as now the mission looks north, from the other side of the roof.

When I open my sketchbook to start afresh I feel the joy of the blank page. The view is north-west, across the unchanged city. A view and a scale that Durrell would have recognised when he sat on these same leads. The view that appealed to the visitors – the first visitors with the first cameras.

There is a magic lantern cast by photography from the past. And when I look north-west to Morfou, I am in its presence – it is a thin ghost standing at my elbow.

Northern Nicosia can sometimes feel desolate and poor, and the silver halide doesn't flatter it. But to me, as I escape into the overview, I can see how exquisite it is, how rich and tranquil. This view is the view of the city as garden, of the arrangement of stones, paths, trees and bougainvillea as they exist at human scale. Of a city, but a modest city whose scale has remained the same for centuries. I share with the photographer from 1906 the same sense that this foreground, that horizon, and this composition, this is Nicosia.

Just not Saray Hotel. Weeks ago it had been said – forget the mosque. Paint from Saray Hotel. Paint from Shakolas Tower. It took one visit to both to establish how much I hate them. This roof, my roof, has no soldiers. No waiters. No air-conditioning. This roof is elemental, and these ancient weathered buttresses make roots to the sacred place, the hub of the great plain. Here I am encircled by flat calm infinity, whose dryness has no hint of the sea. This is a piece of desert in the sky. This is the centre point of the island.

And I have the advantage of being in love. Just as love becomes more able to declare itself with time, with trust and with intimacies shared, so I love this roof-studio, briefly mine. I love the way it feels like a natural thing. I love its lumpiness. And I love its arcana.

There is a stone in the foreground, zigzagged like a crown. What did the Frankish masons mean by placing it here? Its circular zigzags predate and anticipate the circular city walls. Am I surprised that the craft-school and the garden, the corral of rooftops and the gentle fade of the distant Besparmak seem so serene and within its compass? Like a crown it is a ringlet of dominion. It has waited the best part of a millennium for me. It intimates the security of a settled domain.

And yet, over this feudal idyll, this quietly industrious human landscape, is the sky. The unpredictable and changing sky. A great wing of darkening cloud. Invasion. Earthquake. Disaster. Another whole register of feeling.

The enduring, and the instant. This angel trades in time.

***

Dinda has left.

I am exhausted, and alone, but the mission is incomplete. The last of the four, the easiest and most devastating painting awaits.

I turn to the north-east, to the view over St Catherine's, Haydar Pasha, and the island settles into sun-struck stupor.

St Catherine's is to me the most Cypriot of Cypriot buildings. A Gothic box with a single minaret, it is the most mosque-like of the Frankish buildings. A single room. And, as Dinda found, it is the women's mosque.

From my perch on the eastern-most extremity of the roof, amidst the low roofs of the old town, that mosque is transcendent, a sharp finger that pierces the familiar line of the mountains. I conceive the painting as this double dynamic: the mountains dip in a shallow V, as one might pull down on a washing line. The mosque, founded in the city, rises with a Gothic energy that is completed in the skyward, Godward indicator of the minaret. As nature yields, the spirit rises.

In my mind is the idea that this is the contract between the sacred, the city and the world, expressed in the given forms of Nicosia and the Cypriot landscape.

I have made exhaustive, detailed drawings for all the other paintings, but this one begins with a simple sketch, an idea, a dialogue between vectors.

There is something sacramental about this painting. I make order, prepare my skin for the sun, and take off my glasses. To work with my natural sight is the prize that consummates the whole process. I work with extreme slowness. I do more than observe, I must imagine what I see.

The sky is stunned into blue. The temperature is in the high thirties, and windless. Every evening the household squadrons bank and loop around the towers.

The result is that the painting is completely unfanciful. It refers only to the shapes, tones and colours of what is there. There is no sense of history or politics or attrition. It is time spent slowly in the eternal now, like a single rich chord.

All I had to do was to notate the workings of that harmony.
This is the painting that completed me and finished me.
What more is there to say once everything is said?

***

I agreed to sell the paintings so as to leave them in Cyprus, but the
experience only served to reinforce the silence.
        My encounter was with angels, but my words are poor:

the wind
the fear
time
the sacred

Islam does it better.

Michael
Azrael
Israfil
Gabriel

NURSERY TALES

Laila Sumpton

Settle down for your story
your sister is stealing your horse
so she stops being your sister
and you really miss your horse
you learn that you never had a sister
she was just someone close by
as different as land from sky
yet dependent and near
so you go after the pretender
who was always by you as your sister
who planted trees and hollowed wells
who braided you and taught you dance
who speaks a language you won't sing
who has taken her half of the olive tree
and cantered away on your horse
leaping the line she has drawn
and now you wait at the border
carry your rage in your hand

FRAGMENTS FROM AN
ARCHITECTURE OF FORGETTING

Alev Adil

Hotel Amnesia

For over a year I took photographs of all the empty beds I slept in, alone. Sliding the electronic key card into its slot, I felt lucky because life afforded me this certainty; I would always find a safe space, anonymous, hygienic, cleared of the traces of previous occupants, of the inevitability of history. Hotels indulge the fantasy that consequence can be cleaned away by the chambermaid. Tomorrow will wipe the slate clean: two glasses by the bathroom sink, miniature bottles of shampoo and bubble bath, a mini bar and price list, the room service menu, dial nine for an outside line. Every hotel in every city, whatever the view from the window or the décor: from the efficient ugliness of the 70s brutalist Holiday Inn in Niejmegen, to the decaying grandeur of Sarah Bernhardt's room in the Pera Palace in Istanbul, every hotel had the ambience of Hotel Amnesia. I love to watch TV in languages I don't understand. I have learnt to bide my time. Waiting is my newly acquired skill, a talent I value highly – quite an achievement when time is in short supply, is not on my side. I sat in cafés, in Vilnius, Prague, Porto, Seville, writing out fugitive itineraries, although I was never quite certain if I was evading my ghosts or tailing them. The urge to remember and the compulsion to forget are locked in complicity. They are all part of the same haunted clan: the detective, the analyst, the archivist, the academic, the assassin –

all searching for clues, tampering with the evidence, hoping for a conclusion that does not come.

My Favourite Dream

Long after your death I'd wander aimlessly, ride buses to their unfamiliar suburban conclusions, abandoning myself to numbers magic. After several centuries of random searches I knew that I'd find you, that finally the living might speak with and not for the dead. Reparations would be made. The mourning could, would end. The celestial Route Master to armistice would stop for me and everyone I'd ever loved and lost would be there, sailing to oblivion on the upper deck. Sometimes this idea flooded me with a blissful sense of peace, at others it terrified me so completely I'd walk in the rain for miles or hide in the library until the darkness fell. I'd wake up suddenly with the sense of being urgently expected elsewhere. That immobilising panic, a nervous lassitude, you know that feeling that you're too late for a crucial meeting, a vital, forgotten rendezvous; too late for redemption.

When the dream goes well I finally find you again. We meet in the ruins of a cinema, a grand old Gaumont, a 1920s kitsch medieval folly. Snow filters through the collapsed ceiling, motes melting and dancing in the light of the projector. The red velvet curtains are ripped and charred, rich ragged shrouds from a glamorous past. Everything is as devastated and beautiful, as irretrievably strange and lost as Salamis, or Pergamon. Gorgeous filaments of light, sparkling stars and flakes of snow occlude my vision, and although our private civilisation is long gone the screen is still intact, the projector still whirrs into action. We sit side by side and we speak in the silver-nitrate glow.

When I wake up I try desperately to hear your voice again. How I long to hear your voice again. I try to remember what we say to each other, but it's gone. All I can remember is the snow and the whirr of the projector. We're talking so intently that the first time I had the dream I paid no attention to the screen at all, but in subsequent iterations I try to watch, to remember what the film is, because I know there's no possibility of recalling your words, your voice. But you become upset, you want me to look into your beautiful dark eyes, to listen to you. There's nothing I want more myself, and so I abandon myself to your gaze and your scent. I miss your scent. The way I miss your scent breaks my mammal heart.

The Ruined Cinema, the Screen Memory

The ruined cinema is the key to everything; it is the set for the screen that memory is projected upon. The editing strategies of the unconscious provide many technologies of fictionalisation. Events are transferred to a place they didn't occur. Several people are merged into one, or one is substituted for another. Separate experiences are combined. Every time we remember we use psychic technologies analogous to those used in fiction or filmmaking.

A psychic suture is inherent in the act of remembering. The screen memory serves (incompletely or problematically) to repress and omit the objectionable. Memory does not emerge it is formed, edited. We create an archive (fragments of memories) to generate screen memories/narratives; use visual, acoustic, linguistic and melodic metaphors as contiguities to elude closure and allude to indeterminate unarticulations; to explore the processes that determine what we exclude/edit out and what we present as fact or choose to fictionalise. Both the memory and the representation of memory are crafted objects open to interpretation, both have the power to deconstruct and disturb historical and personal narratives as much as to confirm them. The screen is not only a cover but, just as it is in the cinema, it is a plane of projection. 'You projected two fantasies onto one another and turned them into a childhood memory', Freud tells his double, his imaginary analysand. We are the projectors as well as the directors, editors and audience in the cinema of memory.

Perhaps Freud's concept of screen memory is compelling precisely because his interpretation of screen memory refuses closure, the secure finality of a definitive interpretation, which he promises. Screen memory is not only a shroud over a hidden object (subject); it is a process of allusion, a stream of metaphors which provide a contiguity to the zone of the inarticulable. The inarticulable shifts: there is no single unsayable; we are cast into a zone of indeterminacy, an imaginary cinema where we are both projector and sole member of the audience.

We are always divided from the self we see in memory, and any detective work around the identity of that alter ego inevitably alters the ego. The analysis is never complete, the 'meaning' of the memory never fixed. There can be no Final Interpretation to uncover; it will have to be read against all the other analyses created by prior, and subsequent, selves. Whereas the promised pleasures of the detective genre in film and fiction (and of psychoanalysis) speak of a fantasy of order –promising that the criminal will be apprehended, that the Law of the Father will be reinstituted, the mystery will be solved – Freud's detective work here speaks from a more culpable position. Rather than Deleuze and Guattari's forbidding 'priest of interpretation' who is at hand every time 'desire is betrayed, cursed, uprooted from its field of immanence', in *Screen Memories* Freud presents us with the psychoanalyst as far more ambiguous, playful, figure. For while Freud as analyst/a detective 'solves' the murder that has been exiled from articulation, he is also his own analysand/criminal covering his tracks. The detective is closely related to the assassin. The urge to remember and the compulsion to forget are locked in complicity.

A Small Forgotten War

Mine is a small, forgotten war, a modest war even, nothing on a grand scale, some squalid atrocities but no Srebrenicas, more of a sour extended sulk, a long-term corrosion of the soul. I was born into a time of war. I am as old as the Cyprus Problem. I am thousands of years old. The street I was born in has aged centuries in the decades since I left. The memory of the place and the place itself are just so much rubble. That narrow winding back street close to the border in the old walled city is now a trashed slum. The border, that abject septic scar, serves as a monument to war. On both sides of the city we look away. There is a move outwards, towards Kyrenia in the North and Limassol in the South, to dreary new-build suburbs, barbeques in the yard, satellite TV. At the heart of the city there is this wound. Perhaps the Forbidden Zone is almost beautiful in the way it speaks to all of us of our failures, our culpability – unless we choose to forget our own responsibilities for this, our own bloody, tired legacies, and see ourselves as only and always the victims of others. Mine is a small, forgettable war, but all wars give birth to ruins. Ruin eternalises and naturalises destruction, as though it has always been this way, and always will be.

And yet I am not repelled by the festering spaces of the Forbidden Zone. The rust, the stench of rubbish, and the bored conscript soldier boys all shimmer with perverse seduction in the August heat. I am drawn to the dead-end streets that mark the border. I follow the fault line from both sides of the city, hungrily photographing the lines of barbed wire, the observation towers, the bricked-up windows, the bullet-pocked walls. I film my walks until the border guards order me not to. Soldiers are familiar to me, especially the tall, impassive Canadian UN soldiers I remember from the 70s. Crossing the Green Line was something I did every day as a child. I was born into memories of UN blue, of military convoys, checkpoints, rumours of impending war. When the checkpoint opened again, I came back after years away. I kept crossing and re-crossing; the journey was cosy and nostalgic. I liked that walk, my footsteps invisibly scribbling along the scar of the Green Line, past the bus stuck in no man's land for thirty years, past the Ledra Palace Hotel, once the glamorous haunt of visiting ballerinas and spies. The swimming pool I swam in every day in the summer is sandbagged; the hotel now announces itself as a UN exchange point. I like crossing from one side to the other, and back. It doesn't disturb me. War has been home to me. And the sea. Like K says, you can never get tired of watching the sea.

The words 'I don't forget' are emblazoned across Greek Cypriot children's school exercise books. The phrase 'We will not forget' is used in official propaganda on the Turkish Cypriot side. Yet I can make no sense of what is to be remembered or how. All memories become controversial and contested. How to remember? Perhaps more crucially, I ask myself what did I choose to forget? How are we to unstitch the sense we made of it, to wear the scars with equanimity?

The Names of All Her Dolls

All the names of her dolls. She remembered all the names of all her dolls. Their blind faces lined up, a silent jury in the nursery bearing witness to the blue-blurred busyness in the feral shadows of infancy. Memories of childhood are determined by what preoccupied us then. A little girl in Freud's *Screen Memories* remembers all the names of her dolls but no significant family events from that time. Freud contends that these happenstance 'trace-memories' are often contemporaneous with, and speak of, events that profoundly affected us at that time, and are also edited and narrativised to make connections with, and metaphorise later events.

There is only the memory of all the names, her dolls; the rest is a blanket of forgetting, something clean and cold, soft like snow.

But she remembered all the names of all her dolls. Memories are important because there is a constant correlation, as Freud puts it, 'between the psychical significance of an experience and its persistence in the memory.' What are we to make of the elliptical and elusive 'indelible traces' left from our childhoods, 'the relatively small number of isolated recollections of questioning or perplexing significance' that we remember from our earliest years, of the 'banal' fragments that assert an hallucinatory visual insistence? All our earliest memories are sensorial and fragmentary. These shattered pre-narrative vignettes, Freud contends, are not simply unmediated random 'trace memories', but are screen memories that try to articulate the inarticulable, to breach the borders and mark the lineaments of contested territory in the war between the urge to remember and the compulsion to forget.

She remembered all the names of all her dolls, of the blind jury in the nursery. The significance of the screen memory resides precisely in that which is not seen, that which is not shown, but is alluded to. The memory both refers to and suppresses what is significant. The urge to remember and the force of resistance, which wants to forget, do not cancel each other out but reach a compromise.

Memory and the Impossibility of Fidelity
On the last day of his life, in the afternoon, Lysandros whispered his last poem about Apollo, the gleaming warrior now disguised as a thousand reeling birds, and slipped irretrievably from the spoken to the written word. His funeral was as theatrical, dignified and unconventional as he was: the gilt splendour of the Greek Orthodox Church in Camden, with all its traditional incense and ritual but also with, controversially, unbelievers, heathens, Turkish Cypriots reading elegies. I'm not sure who persuaded the Greek Orthodox priest to allow such a heresy. Mustafa made sure that

Lysandros was buried in Highgate cemetery as he'd wished. The flowers were white. He'd written: 'Anoint me with white flowers when I lose my blessed breath', although there was no 'crown of white flowers, jasmine, held by a golden thread'.

I can't quite capture the grain of his voice, the cadences of his speech, the swoop of a downward inflection at the end of each line, but I can still hear the sound of the handful of earth each mourner flung on the coffin. Years later, when Mustafa opened the tidy little suitcase that held Lysandros' work, poems spilled out, yellow pages like doves, jaundiced with age, or bleached ravens. Silence flocked and filled the room; the air was heavy, as if rippled by invisible moths. His words are a challenge to that silence, if not a refutation of it, while I am putting words on a dead man's eyes. In whose shiny currency are my words minted? Where is the most unjust betrayal? Mourning erases the lost ones, translates them always and only as absence.

A Minute Taker at the Conference of Birds: On Sufi Symmetry
Something that Aamer wrote reminded me of a time I haven't lived, a place I haven't seen, under an open slate-grey sky. I came to the tower (the blue plaque read 'Rapunzel cried here') at dusk, in the autumn. Don't ask me when, I can't remember whether we wore our trousers tight or flared that year, whether we dressed like gypsies, soldiers or porn stars, whose song played everywhere, leaked out in every café and bar. It was in the time of forty days – the measure of time they mark you out with when you are born, when you give birth, when you are lost in the wilderness, after you die. It was that kind of time, which is all the time in world; is no time: the time you measure when everything no longer makes sense.

I could see all the world from the tower. All the world I could see was empty. There was no one but me. I sang, and the echoes orchestrated me, the wind carried me across the desert. No one heard me. I waited. I waited for the one who tracks my invisible footprints. I waited for the one who knows my name, who comes to find me. Whoever you are, I kept watch for you, a tiny figure on the horizon. Believe me, it was a cinematic moment. No one filmed it. No one disturbed the elegant line of the horizon but the great flocks of birds that filled the sky. That winter they flew south at a distance: geese, flamingos, little birds whose names I didn't know. I'd come well prepared for solitude and lots of walking, but my knowledge of ornithology was, still is, nil.

I shared the tower with birds. My room was filled with ravens and doves. They cooed. They clawed. They crowded me. I remembered what Aamer wrote, that the Sufi sage had said the doves were our nobler feelings, the ravens our anger, our fear, our doubt. The Sufi said I must free the doves, let them fly free, but should keep the ravens locked in or they'd only return with their malevolence redoubled, to shatter the windows, demolish the tower.

In truth, I wanted them all gone. They blurred my vision, got caught in my hair. They deafened me. I tried. I did as he said. But the doves (oh, in my darker moments I see only albino pigeons) kept coming back to roost, breeding in the eaves enthusiastically, back in the overcrowded room again. The ravens grew thin, grew restive, they pecked at me, ate the doves' eggs, hatched conspiracies in the darker corners of the room. I lived in a flurry of feathers: birds battering to get out, birds battering to get back in. And a lot of shit.

Let them all fly. I gave up. I left the tower, climbed down Rapunzel's dead plait, avoiding the thorns that blinded her lover. I set out across the sand. The horizon was a shifting curve ahead, the tower an inky black landmark behind me. I walked my words across the desert, letting the wind delete each phrase easefully with sibilant breaths before a sentence could reach any conclusion. I did not mind. It was a kind of mercy. I walked to find a story, to draw a line and mark a path to the sea. It was a journey. It was a map, a map of forgetting.

The birds were my compass. I knew I'd smell the salt, scent the open sea, long before I reached the shore. I'd hear the scream of seagulls. I'd know I had arrived. A vulture kept me company. We shared the same dry sense of humour (useful in a desert). When I despaired, he'd reassure me that he'd always stick with me until the end. Then further. When the time came he'd polish my bones, make them pretty. I was grateful. We must strive to keep up appearances, to maintain certain aesthetic standards. We must look our best irrespective of circumstance, despite the puzzling absence of a camera crew or paparazzi. After weeks of waiting we doubted we'd ever find the coast, and he tried to comfort me. 'Maybe you should give up on the ocean thing. Maybe that's too excessive an ambition for the season. Why don't we see if we can make it to the Salt Lake for the annual Conference of Birds?' A good idea, surely someone in that mirage of flamingos and nightingales, of eagles and swans, surely one of the delegates would have news? They'd know if there was Someone – the Someone who was waiting not knowing I'd been delayed and lost my way, the One who had set out to find me.

Back in the tower the ravens and the doves flourished and mated. A new species, a sleek grey ghost-raven, was born. Invisible at dusk and dawn, on a grey winter's afternoon, nameless equivocal creatures, they sang all of happiness, all of sadness, violence and tenderness; all of it and all at once. What is there to say of these mercury-spun creatures with the habitual stealth of London's December afternoons, who steal the day from you before you are properly awake, who invade your dreams masquerading as presentiments and omens? They cannot be caged. They cannot be trained and tamed. They'll only sing when they feel like it.

Put your hands on this cage of bone. Feel them beating to

escape from my ribs, a burst of wings, of feathered wildness, a beautiful, terrible song. Send for the hawk to hunt them. Let it swoop and circle its prey mercilessly: a gorgeous symmetry.

STANDING IN FRONT
OF THE LEDRA PALACE

Diomedes Koufteros

He must have visited Saint Hilarion castle, this architect who designed Ledra Palace hotel. These arches with their sharp, steep curves, pointed in the middle; these sculpted shapes through the windows, of leaves and gothic flowers, are reminiscent of that hull, that empty shell. And next to and above the main entrance, with a sign made of seven or eight separate letters in pseudo-gothic or neo-gothic or seventies-style type that spell ΛΗΔΡΑ ΠΑΛΑΣ, in Greek, by the corner of the balcony on the second or third floor, a spectacular sun is etched into the yellow sandstone (or is it ochre?). Only half a sun, though, after some shell, sometime in 1974, struck the balcony pillar from the inside, half of the shrapnel carving the sandstone, half of it blasting towards the room. The glass surely must have shattered, the railing splintered, and through the subsequent renovations by the UN all that's left on this here balcony, or next to it, above the main entrance on the second or third floor, is half a medieval sun, carved in stone in a single blast that must have been terrific and terrifying to whoever was staying in that deluxe room at the time, if anyone.

I was to attend, one day, some rare event or other at the ex-hotel, now UN headquarters, where hundreds of UN soldiers, men and women – but mostly men – stay. I hadn't seen the doorbell at the gate, so I started yelling something annoying like 'Hello?' repeatedly, and loudly enough that the most beautiful blue eyes with short dirty-blonde hair and half-unbuttoned UN fatigues came to open the gate, a bit exasperated at having been rushed out of the loo.

These men, these boys, what do they do at the end of their day, so far from the United Kingdom and Argentina, Bosnia Herzegovina and Bolivia, or wherever the hell they're from? Do they go to sleep glistening with sweat from the hot Nicosia sun of the day that soaked in the ochre sandstone, lying alone next to the half-sun and the 'RIP Charlie' etchings?

Oh, I'd like to know.

SHADES OF A CITY

Mary Anne Zammit

Between night and day.
The city is closed, divided by cold gates.
In the midst of silence and lines of despair.
Walls of silence sending instructions without meaning.
Only feelings of captivity.

I see you every day standing at the other side.
Hidden behind the line.
While your lover waits for you.

Last night I had a dream and you were there.
Walking freely, no borders suffocating you.
And you smiled as the skies watched over you.
Finally, the time has come for freedom.
That is how I see it.
I close my eyes.
So that when you pass you will tell me what it means to breathe
    freely and forget all about barriers and chains which bind you.
Silence reigns over me.
And now I am prepared for the new scene.
A new dawn.

GLOSSARY

Ayo: Yes (Armenian).

Bahr: The sea (Arabic).

Bakshish: An Ottoman term for a tip or small gift.

Boyunbagi: An Ottoman necktie, introduced in the westernization of the Ottoman Empire during the nineteenth century *Tanzimat* (Reform) period.

Büyük Han: The largest *caravanserai* in Cyprus, it was built in Nicosia by the Ottomans in 1572 following their conquest of the island.

Deniz: The sea (Turkish).

Dragoman: A dragoman (derived from *tarjuman*) was an Ottoman interpreter, translator, and official guide fluent in Arabic, Persian, Turkish, and European languages.

Efharistó: Thank you in Greek.

EOKA: Ethniki Organosis Kyprion Agoniston was a nationalist paramilitary organisation formed in 1955 to end British colonial rule and unite Cyprus with Greece.

Evet! Yaa... işte böyle: Yes! So... that's how it is (Turkish).

Haydi: Let's in Turkish.

Hodjas: Islamic term indicating a scholar or teacher.

Jubbeh: Long coat-like outer garment worn by men in the Ottoman era.

Kufta: An Ottoman garment.

Kyria: Respectful term of address to a woman (Greek).

Mahalle: Neighbourhood (Turkish).

Πατσάλα (patsala): Calico cat (Greek).

Qattusa tal-madonna: Calico cat (Maltese).

Rum: Historically an Ottoman term for subjects who belonged to the Greek Orthodox Church (referring to the Byzantine and Holy-Roman Empire) used by Turks and Turkish-speaking Cypriots to describe Greek-speaking Cypriots and distinguish them from *Yunanlı*, Greeks.

Tarjuman: Translator (Arabic).

Θάλασσα (thalassa): The sea (Greek).

TMT: Türk Mukavemet Teşkilatı (Turkish Resistance Organisation) was a nationalist paramilitary organisation formed in 1958, in response to the formation and activities of EOKA, that promoted the partition of Cyprus and the union of the Turkish-speaking part of the island with Turkey.

Rayahs: A non-Muslim subject of the Ottoman Empire.

Υψίστους διδασκάλους (Upsistous Didaskalous): High school teachers (Greek).

ABOUT THE EDITORS

Alev Adil is a performance artist–poet and academic who has performed internationally, including at Tate Britain and the British Museum. Her poetry has been included in numerous anthologies of Cypriot poetry in English, Greek and Turkish, and has been translated into eight languages. She has a PhD in multimedia poetics from Central Saint Martin's, and has extensive experience of teaching Visual Culture, Literature and Creative Writing at BA and MA level in universities in the UK and abroad.

Aydın Mehmet Ali is an intellectual activist, writer and translator. She is the director and founder of Literary Agency Cyprus and co-director and founder of Cyclists Across Barriers. Her work is taught at universities around the world and has appeared in international anthologies, journals and magazines. Her publications include *Turkish Cypriot Identity in Literature*, *Turkish Speaking Communities & Education – No Delight* and *Forbidden Zones*.

Bahriye Kemal is a poet, writer and academic. Her creative and academic work has appeared in various magazines, anthologies, journals and books. She is co-editor of *Visa Stories: Experiences between Law and Migration*, and author of *Writing Cyprus: Postcolonial and Partitioned Literatures of Space and Place*. She is a lecturer in Postcolonial Contemporary Literatures at the University of Kent.

Maria Petrides is an independent writer, editor and translator. She has contributed to magazines, anthologies and art publications, and participated in writer-in-residencies in New York City, Nicosia, Istanbul, Helsinki, Rio de Janeiro and Geneva. She is co-founder of artist group pick nick, the author of *A Book of Small Things* and assistant editor for *Evripides Zantides' Semiotics: Visual Communication II*.

ABOUT THE CONTRIBUTORS

Anthony Anaxagorou is an award-winning British–born Cypriot poet, fiction writer, essayist, publisher and poetry educator. He has published several volumes of poetry, including *After the Formalities* (forthcoming 2019), a spoken-word EP and a collection of short stories.

Shola Balogun is a poet, playwright, filmmaker, and author of *The Wrestling of Jacob* and *Praying Dangerously: The Cry of Blind Bartimaeus*. He has an MA in Theatre Arts from the University of Ibadan, Nigeria, and has contributed poetry, essays and dramatic criticism to various magazines, anthologies and journals.

Elisa Bosio is a writer of Italian–Lebanese origin who was born and raised in Saudi Arabia. She co-founded and served as assistant editor of *Flair: The Literary Magazine*, a student journal of literature and the arts in Cyprus, where she now lives.

Norbert Bugeja is senior lecturer in Postcolonial Studies at the Mediterranean Institute, University of Malta. He has published two poetry collections in Maltese, *Nartici* (shortlisted for the National Book Award: Poetry 2017) and *Bliet*, which was awarded second place at the National Book Award: Poetry 2010. One volume of his work, *South of the Kasbah*, is available in English translation.

Antoine Cassar is a Maltese poet and translator. His book-length poem *Erbghin Jum* (*40 Days*, EDE) won the National Book Prize in 2018 and was shortlisted for the Gdánsk European Poet of Freedom Award 2020. Other works include *Passaport*, published in eleven languages and adapted for theatre in Malta, France and Belgium, and *Merhba*, winner of the 2009 United Planet Writing Prize.

Sherry Charlton has a degree in Psychology from Cardiff University and has lectured in social sciences. For forty years she has taught children of all ages with a range of learning, social, emotional and behavioural difficulties. Inspired by her experiences and memories of living in Nicosia as a child, this is her first foray into creative writing.

Hakan Djuma is a Turkish-speaking Cypriot and environmental scientist. His poetry has been published in the journal *Isirgan*, and he was awarded second prize by the Cyprus Writers Association in 2010 for his short story 'Kuzev,' which was also translated into Greek and published in the magazine *Nea Epochy*.

Dinda Fass is a visual artist and writer based in Edinburgh. Her practice spans across photography, video, text and poetry. Her work has been screened as part of Glasgow International Art at the Museum of Modern Art and in Edinburgh. She spent 2015 in Nicosia, where her photographs were exhibited in Nicosia in 2018 as part of 'the island' series at the Museum of the Pancyprian Gymnasium.

Sevina Floridou is a historic preservation architect and independent researcher. She writes about historic building conservation, water research and historic sites caught in disputed landscapes. Her work has been published in books and journals, and includes *Voroklini Waterfront* (co-written with M. Danou), which received the Cyprus State Exceptional Architecture Award.

Marianna Foka was born in Nicosia. She has a BA in History and Philosophy of Art from the University of Kent and an MA in Cultural Policy and Management from City University, London. She was one of seventy-five poets from around the world included in the honorary poetic collection *Leonard Cohen: You're Our Man.* Her work has been published internationally in magazines and journals.

Gür Genç (Korkmazel) is a poet, writer and translator. He was born in Pafos in 1969. After the division in 1974, he and his family were evacuated, resettling in Northern Cyprus in Mesaoria. He has translated Taner Baybars, John Clare and Lawrence Durrell into Turkish, and has six published books of poetry and three collections of short stories. His work has been translated into English, Greek, German, French, Dutch and Lithuanian.

Melissa Hekkers is a journalist and author. She focuses on silenced communities and refugees, and also teaches creative writing. Her publications include *Crocodile*, which won the Cyprus State Illustration Award 2007; *Flying Across Red Skies*, for which she was nominated for the Cyprus State Literary Award 2012; *Pupa*, and a free-verse poetry collection, *Come-forth*.

Kivanc Houssein is a Turkish Cypriot living in London. He is a business owner and amateur writer contributing articles for various websites.

Andriana Ierodiaconou was born in Nicosia. She has a degree in Biochemistry from Oxford University. Her poetry collections include *Of Koma Yialou* and *The Trawler*. Her poems have been translated into English, French, Swedish, Turkish and Lithuanian. She is also the author of two novels in English, *Margarita's Husband* and *The Women's Coffee Shop*.

Erato Ioannou was born in Pafos and lives in Nicosia. She writes in Greek and English. Her work has appeared in literary journals and anthologies in Cyprus, Greece, Romania and the UK. Erato is a working mum of two, a wife, a writer, and an associate editor at *In Focus* literary journal.

Jacqueline Jondot is a retired professor of English literature now based in Lyon, France. Her academic writing includes a 3rd cycle thesis on *Orlando* by Virginia Wolf and a PhD thesis on Middle Eastern Arab Anglophone authors. She translated *Outremer* by Nabil Saleh into French, and her photography work of Cairene *mashrabiyyas* and Egyptian revolution graffiti have been publicly exhibited.

Stavros Stavrou Karayanni is associate professor of English in the Department of Humanities at the European University Cyprus. He explores issues related to Middle Eastern dance, culture, gender and sexuality. He is author of *Dancing Fear and Desire: Race, Sexuality and Imperial Politics in Middle Eastern Dance*, co-author of *Sexual Interactions: The Social Construction of Atypical Sexual Behaviors*, and co-editor of *Vernacular Worlds, Cosmopolitan Imagination*. He is managing editor of the journal *Cadences*.

Maria Kitromilidou was born in Athens. She is a law graduate of Kings College London and London School of Economics. She has lived most of her life in Limassol, Cyprus, where she is currently managing partner of a group of companies providing legal and consultancy services to an international clientele.

Diomedes Koufteros is an actor. He has played the MC in *Cabaret* and Perre Ubu in *Ubu Roi*, and has produced theatre including *Evelyn Evelyn* and *The Overcoat*. He has taught theatre at the University of Nicosia and the Satirikon theatre. He worked as an advisor for EACEA's Creative Europe programme, and was the artistic director for *Greater Nicosia 2021*, Nicosia's bid for the European Youth Capital.

Dize Kükrer studied Architecture and Fine Art at the University of Plymouth, UK. Her work is concerned with time and space, and their relationship to memory. She completed an MA in Interdisciplinary Design at Frederick University in 2016, and is currently an assistant curator at Arkın University of Creative Arts and Design.

Bahir Laattoe was born in South Africa, where he fought against apartheid. Whilst teaching English and Geography in a township school he become involved in activism, including the youth struggle, the community struggle, the trade union struggle and the struggle for non-racial sport. As a result of his political work, he had to leave South Africa and settled in London, where he continues to be politically active.

Lisa Majaj is the author of *Geographies of Light* and co-editor of numerous collections. Her writing has been published across Europe, the Middle East and the US, most recently in *Making*

Mirrors: Writing/Righting by Refugees. Her work has also been featured in non-literary venues, including the photography exhibition *Aftermath: The Fallout of War – America and the Middle East* at Harn Museum of Art, Florida in 2016.

Despina Michaelidou was born in Limassol. They are a post-graduate student of Gender Studies at the University of Cyprus, and have a bachelor's degree in Sociology from the University of Aegean, Lesbos. Their interests include genders, sexualities, desires and bodies through intersectional, artistic, feminist, anarchist, antimilitarist and queer collective initiatives and performances.

Haji Mike is a dub-poet, recording artist, DJ, radio broadcaster and associate professor in Communications at the University of Nicosia. He has been making music since 1990, and in 2017 founded the band the HighGate Rockers in Nicosia with four others. Haji Mike has toured France, Greece, Ireland, Jamaica, Japan, Morocco, Portugal, South Africa, the USA, the UK and extensively throughout Cyprus.

Christodoulos Moisa is an award-winning poet and artist. He was born in 1948 to immigrant Cypriot parents. Moisa has published two novels, a collection of short stories, six poetry collections and the critically acclaimed long poem *The Desert.* Moisa lives and works in Whanganui New Zealand.

Tinashe Mushakavanhu is a writer, editor and scholar from Zimbabwe. He co-edited *State of the Nation: Contemporary Zimbabwean Poetry* and *Visa Stories: Experiences Between Law and Migration.* He has a PhD in English from the University of Kent and is lead researcher for Reading Zimbabwe.

Nora Nadjarian is a writer and poet. She has won recognition in international competitions including the Commonwealth Short Story Competition and the Seán Ó Faoláin Short Story Prize. Her short story collections include *Ledra Street* and *Selfie*. Her work has also been included in the books *A River of Stories*, *Best European Fiction 2011*, *Being Human* and *Capitals*.

Argyro Nicolaou is a writer, scholar and filmmaker. She has a PhD in Comparative Literature and Critical Media Practice from Harvard University. Argyro's first narrative short, *In Half*, about an artist's work being censored, was screened in festivals in Cyprus, Romania, and the US. She has received numerous fellowships and awards, and her writing has been published in journals.

Münevver Özgür Özersay is an architect and creative director of Miro Designroom, a bathroom design and material supply company. She has a PhD from the Eastern Mediterranean University, Faculty of Architecture, where she was a full-time academic staff member at the Department of Interior Architecture from 2012 – 2018.

Shereen Pandit is a lawyer, lecturer, political activist and trade unionist. She came to the UK from South Africa in political exile and obtained a PhD in law. Pandit's work, which includes the novel *A Burnt Child*, the short story collection *Waiting for Fidel in the Springtime* and a collection (prose, poetry, memoir), *Trafalgar: The Golden Years*, has been widely published and translated into various languages.

Yiannis Papadakis is professor of Social Anthropology at the Department of Social and Political Sciences, University of Cyprus. He is author of *Echoes from the Dead Zone: Across the Cyprus*

Divide and co-editor of *Cypriot Cinemas: Memory, Conflict and Identity in the Margins of Europe*. His work focuses on borders, nationalism, memory, historiography, history education, cinema, migration and social democracy.

Rachael Pettus is a teacher of English as a second language. She is co-founder of the Caritas Project, the Learning Refuge (a language and integration centre in Paphos that works with the area's refugee population) and of Μαζί/Together/معا, a grassroots language and integration organisation.

Zoe Piponides teaches English in Larnaca. Her work has been commended in competitions including the Alan Sillitoe Memorial Competition, *Ink Pellet*, *Poetry Review* and the National Academy of Writing. Her poems have appeared in the international publications *The Font Journal*, *Pickled Body*, *Huffington Post* and the *Eighty-Four* anthology.

Angus Reid writes, paints and makes films. His poetry includes 'The Gift', 'White Medicine' and 'The Book of Days'; his films include *Brotherly Love*, *The Ring* (Best Central European Feature Documentary 2004), and 'Primary School Musical!'. He has painted Nicosia since 1985, culminating in the exhibition 'Vision of Nicosia' in collaboration with Dinda Fass at the Bedestan and Gloria Gallery.

Caroline Rooney is a writer, filmmaker and university professor. Born in Zimbabwe and currently based in the UK, her projects over the last decade have involved collaborations with arts activists in Palestine, Lebanon, Egypt and Cyprus. Her poems have appeared in *In Protest: 150 Poems for Human Rights* and *Over Land, Over Sea: Poems for Those Seeking Refuge*.

Jenan Selçuk is a poet, writer, freelance translator and editor. He is a member of the Writers Union in the South and is on the board of the Artists and Writers Union in the North of Cyprus. He was the publisher of the underground journal, *Isırgan (Nettle)*. His poetry collections include *Kaza*, *Haz* and *Şeytanrı*, and his works have been translated into ten languages.

Salamis Aysegul Sentug is a writer from Cyprus. She holds MA degrees in both Philosophy and Philosophy of Art and Literature, and is currently pursuing a PhD on the Contemporary Novel at the University of Kent, where she teaches Creative Writing. Parallel to her academic publications, she has published poetry and short stories in various magazines and three travelogues, and her first novel is in progress.

Constantia Soteriou was born in Nicosia. Her first book, *Aishe Goes on Vacation*, won the Athens Prize for Literature in 2016 and was shortlisted for the Greece National Book Awards. *Voices Made of Soil*, her second novel, was shortlisted for the Cyprus National Book Awards. She writes plays for the Cyprus Theatre Organization, amongst others, and has had numerous short stories published in anthologies and Greek and Cypriot literature magazines.

Stephanos Stephanides is a poet, literary and cultural critic, ethnographer and translator. His publications include *Translating Kali's Feast* and *Blue Moon in Rajasthan and Other Poems*, and his poetry has been translated into ten languages. Stephanos is currently a professor of Comparative Literature at the University of Cyprus.

Laila Sumpton is a member of the Keats House Poets and an associate writer at Spread the Word. She facilitates projects in hospitals, museums, libraries, galleries, parks, schools and universities. She co-founded the refugee and migrant poetry collective 'Bards Without Borders', is Writing Program Leader at Ministry of Stories, and has performed her work across the UK. She is published in several anthologies and magazines, and is currently working on her first poetry collection.

Christos Tsiailis is an English teacher, triathlete and writer. His publications include poems and short stories in English and Greek literary magazines. He has won numerous prizes, including first prize in a recent UNESCO poetry contest about the return of the Parthenon marbles to Greece. His books include *Throwing Dice on A Chessboard*, *The Green Divorce*, *Klotho Surfaces*, and short story collection ΨΩΜΙ (*Bread*).

Adrian Woolrich-Burt is currently studying social and political science at the London School of Economics. He has written on subjects including the NATO interventions in Yugoslavia and the legality of the post-9/11 wars.

Anthie Zachariadou studied law in Nicosia and works as an executive director. Her short stories have been published online and in anthologies, and her plays include *Caterina: The Last Queen of Cyprus* (United Solo Festival, 2017), *Eleonora of Cyprus* (2016) and *Bacon/Freud* (Cyprus Theatre Week 2017, Athens). In 2018, *CON*, a play written in collaboration with Marios Nicolaou, won first prize at Reading Festival, Athens, and ran at Apo Koinou Theatre, Greece.

Marilena Zackheos studied philosophy, creative writing and English literature in the USA and the UK. She is director of the Cyprus Center for Intercultural Studies and assistant professor of Social Sciences at the University of Nicosia. Her writing is concerned with postcolonial literary and cultural studies, psychoanalysis, trauma, gender and sexuality. She has one published poetry collection, *Carmine Lullabies*.

Mary Anne Zammit is a graduate in Social Work, Probation Services and Diplomatic Studies, and author of novels in Maltese and English. Her poetry has been published in numerous publications including *The Strand Book for International Poetry*, *Literature Today*, *Taj Mahal Review*, *International Contemporary Poetry* and the *International Collection of Poetry*.

ACKNOWLEDGEMENTS

This book has been inspired by the activities of Literary Agency Cyprus (LAC). LAC is a women-led literary and arts movement founded in Nicosia by Aydın Mehmet Ali. It challenges the dominant racist literary discourses, which deny the multicultural, multilingual, multifaith nature and herstories and literatures of Cyprus.

LAC is a collaborative venture which includes many of the contributors to this book, including the editors, Maria Petrides, Alev Adil and Bahriye Kemal. Aydın Mehmet Ali brought together fifteen like-minded women who she had crossed paths with during her years of walking, writing and cycling, in Nicosia in August 2013, in the Forbidden Zone. They have gone on to organise projects using literature and the arts to foster solidarity, acknowledge differences and challenge dominant and official discourses, as they break taboos, in and through Cyprus.

Since 2013, LAC has organised various projects on the island and internationally led by various participants, all of who have contributed to shaping this anthology. LAC aims to provide services helping writers to bring their work to publishing standards. It takes the literatures of Cyprus onto the streets, to venues and audiences beyond the usual in Cyprus, and onto the international arena, including the events Mediterranean Fractures I and II (UK and Malta) and White Flags: Bridges within and Between Lebanon and Cyprus (UK and Palestine).

As editors our very special thanks to Amjad Abujayyab, Nadia

Kornioti, Natalie Georgalla, Buğu M. Riza and Bryony Blood Smyth for their dedicated admin support, ideas and care over the last four years, during the journey of this book.

LAC is indebted to the following workshop leaders and assistants, photographers, filmmakers, visual artists, city walkers, cyclists, press and television journalists for their generous, unflinching support and professionalism in making the *Nicosia Beyond Barriers* project such a success across the island and beyond. LAC is also indebted to all the contributors and participants to our successful projects since its inception in 2013. This anthology is the culmination of all their energies. They include Aydın Mehmet Ali (project manager), Agnieszka Rakoczy, Alev Adil, Bahriye Kemal, Maria Petrides, Andriana Ierodiakonou, Batu Palmer, Eleni Skarparis, Erato Ioannou-Moustaka, Filiz Bilen, Kamil Saldun, Konstantinos Konstantinou, Lisa Suhair Majaj, Maria A. Ioannou, Marilena Zackheos, Marios Epaminondas, Miranda Hoplaros, Münevver Özgür, Nicoletta Demetriou, Nurtane Karagil, Rachael Pettus, Sholeh Zahraei, Stephanos Stephanides, Tina Adamidou, Valentine Stavrou, Anna Stelmach and Hakan Çakmak.

Our thanks to Nicosia Municipality Arts Centre (NiMAC) and the Pierides Foundation for selecting the project for the 'Treasure Island' (2014) and hosting the readings, performances and film shows in South Nicosia, and to Rüstem Bookshop for the reading in North Nicosia. Our appreciation to the Centre for Visual Arts and Research (CVAR) for hosting our 'Women Walk the Night' workshop, and to the Stelios Foundation, that recognised the potential of the anthology and supported it from the start.

We thank Elizabeth Briggs from Saqi Books for her valued expertise in bringing out the best in each piece, and being receptive to our suggestions. Together, we have learned.

We owe much to the Commonwealth Foundation for supporting the anthology and to Emma D'Costa and Janet Steel for their confidence in the anthology and for removing barriers.

Above all, thank you to our followers, audiences and those who ensure the success of our events and projects by showing up in large numbers.

And finally, to our loved ones who put up with us...

CREDITS

Norbert Bugeja's 'Ledra' first appeared in the collection *South of the Kasbah* (Midsea books, 2015)

Melissa Hekkers's 'Island in the Sun' was written based on interviews carried out with migrants in Nicosia in 2015–2016. It was part of the exhibition 'Island in the Sun' by Maren Wickwire and Melissa Hekkers, first presented at the Goethe Institute Zypern as part of the Buffer Fringe Performing Arts Festival. All names have been changed to secure the privacy of interviewees.

Andriana Ierodiaconou's 'The Heart of Nicosia' was first published in Greek in *Tis Kómis Ayialou* (Nicosia: Kochlias Press, 1982). The English translation was first published in the Graham House Review No.11, Spring 1988, Colgate University Press, NY; Greek and English versions were reprinted in *The Trawler* (Nicosia: Moufflon Publications, 2016).

Jacqueline Jondot's 'Why Are Green Lines Called Green?' was first published in *Cadences: A Journal of Literature and the Arts in Cyprus*, issue 11 Fall 2015

Stavros Stavrou Karayanni's 'Gardening Desire' is an excerpt from Karayanni, S. S. (2018), 'Anamnesis and Queer Poe(/li)tics: Dissident Sexualities and the Erotics of Transgression in Cyprus', *Journal of Greek Media & Culture*, 4:2, 239-254.

Bahriye Kemal's 'Introduction' draws on ideas from Kemal, B. *Writing Cyprus: Postcolonial and Partitioned Literatures of Place and Space* (Routledge, 2019).

Münevver Özgür Özersay's 'Buzzing Bees in My House' was first written in Nicosia in Turkish and printed in *Gaile* on 19 March 2014. It was translated into English by the author and with the help of Aydın Mehmet Ali for a reading event at Home for Cooperation, 25 April 2015.

Yiannis Papadakis's 'The Story of the Dead Zone and The Language of the Dead Zone' are edited excepts from his book *Echoes from the Dead Zone: Across the Cyprus Divide* (London: IB Tauris, 2005).

Stephanos Stephanides's 'Broken Heart' was first published in *Blue Moon in Rajasthan and Other Poems* (Nicosia: Kochlias, 2005).

Stephanos Stephanides's 'Rhapsody on the Dragoman' was first published in R. Vanita's *India and the World: Postcolonialism, Translation and Indian Literature: Essay in Honour of Harish Trivedi* (New Delhi: Pencraft International, 2014).

Marilena Zackheos's 'Within the Walls' first appeared in the collection *Carmine Lullabies* (Nicosia: Bookworm, 2016).

THE COMMONWEALTH FOUNDATION

The Commonwealth Foundation was established by Heads of Government in support of the idea that the Commonwealth is as much an association of peoples as it is of governments. It is a unique, stand-alone multilateral organisation; it is funded by and reports to governments, which have given it a mandate to support civil society. The Foundation is dedicated to advancing people's participation in promoting responsive, effective and accountable governance so that ultimately their quality of life is improved. The Foundation is the Commonwealth's agency for arts and culture.

COMMONWEALTH WRITERS

Commonwealth Writers is the cultural initiative of the Commonwealth Foundation. It inspires and connects writers and storytellers across the world, bringing personal stories to a global audience. Commonwealth Writers believes in the transformative power of creative expression in all its forms. It works with local and international partners to identify and deliver a wide range of cultural projects. The activities take place in Commonwealth countries, but its community is global.